CHRISTMAS IN COOPERSTOWN

BY PETER J. MURGIO

Cover Design by Kevin Craig
Interior Design by Pamela Morrell

Hardcover book: 979-8-9872440-0-5
Softcover ISBN: 979-8-9872440-1-2
Ebook ISBN: 979-8-9872440-2-9

Published by

1620 SW 5th Avenue
Pompano Beach, Florida 33060
(954)788-4775
editors@editingforauthors.com
dragontreebooks.com

Dedication

Dedicated to my dearest wife, Kathy, my inspiration not just for writing but for living, and to Cooperstown, a special place where our lives became one over fifty years ago.

Contents

CHAPTER ONE
I Love You in Heaven

When Blake Anderson woke up in his third-floor apartment on Flushing Avenue, he looked around the room and saw a pile of dirty laundry. It was Saturday, which meant housekeeping chores for him and Cooper. The dreaded trip to the laundromat involving lots of pre-spotting and folding piles of "stuff" was here again. Not too long ago, Blake had no idea what pre-spotting even was. But things were different now. Amy was gone; it was just Cooper and him: the dynamic duo, as Cooper dubbed them.

Not anxious to begin laundry day, he rolled over and stared up at the ceiling for a moment and remembered what should be un-remembered.

*****

It had been a September sunny morning with a fresh, clean breeze and blue-blue skies. Blake remembered it would be a big day for him and his wife. They were both on their way to the top but still had a lot of territory to cover before getting a bite out of the Big Apple.

He sprang from his bed and headed towards the shower while Amy went into the other room to hustle Cooper, their eight-year-old son, out of bed.

Blake surveyed his closet and decided on his new blue pinstripe. He said to himself, "Very bankerish, perfect for the occasion." And the occasion was the launch of his first IPO deal at JP Morgan. It was not only a big deal dollar-wise; it was a big deal for his career. He would be one of the youngest in his firm to pull off this kind of transaction. It had been months in the making, and today was the culmination of all that work. He would take a bow in front of the senior management and be recognized by his peers.

It was also a big day for his darling Amy. She was having her second interview at her law firm for the junior partner position. It was between her and one other associate; this interview was critical. Amy walked into Cooper's spacious bedroom with a park view.

"Come on, big guy, it's time to get up. School awaits." Amy sniffed and curled up her nose.

"Mom, I don't feel good. And I got sick last night."

"Yeah, I see, buddy." She reached down and felt his forehead. A touch warm. This was the last thing Amy needed this morning—and her poor baby looked as gray as his sheets. "Oh, Coop, I'm so sorry. Does your tummy hurt?"

"Yeah, but not so much now. I didn't sleep all night."

She winced. "Why didn't you come to get Mommy or Daddy?"

"I did, but you and Dad were sleeping so nice that I didn't want to wake you."

"Aww, you are such a sweetie." She walked to the bathroom and returned with a thermometer. "Now, let me take your temperature." Amy again felt Cooper's forehead as she waited for the thermometer to register. "Hmm, 99 degrees. Well, that isn't too much to worry about."

"Mom, I don't want to go to school today. I feel awful, and I don't want to get sick there. The kids will make fun of me."

"Let me call Mary Lou and see if she could come and stay with you today."

"Thanks, Mom. I love you."

Amy walked into their sizeable gracious living room, also facing Central Park. This room was her favorite: sleek designer furniture, floor-to-ceiling windows, and a killer view. The park was still lush and green with their bird's-eye view of the treetops. Soon it would unveil its autumn majesty—her favorite season. Amy didn't regret renting this place furnished since neither she nor Blake had the time to pick out and buy their own. And besides, they probably couldn't afford to buy this kind of stuff anyway. She knew that someday they would move and then take the time to purchase their own furniture. Amy called Mary Lou, their regular babysitter, but there was no answer. She then tried two others, who were already engaged for the day. Now she was getting nervous. This was an important day for both Blake and her.

She walked into the master bedroom, where Blake was selecting a tie. "Blake, we have a problem. Cooper doesn't feel well. He got sick last night and has a stomachache."

"Does he need to go to the doctor?"

"I don't know, probably not. He ate a lot of candy yesterday. Went to that birthday party Saturday, and you should have seen the goodie bag he came home with. I found all the wrappers in his trashcan, so it's probably just that. I tried calling Mary Lou and a couple of other sitters, but no luck."

She sat on the corner of their king-size bed, and Blake walked over and sat next to her. They looked at each other. Both of them were flat out today. Finally, Amy said: "Look, I'll call the office and tell them Cooper is sick. Maybe they will postpone the interview until tomorrow."

"No, don't do that, Amy. That would be looked at negatively. It's hard enough for women without kids to be partners in a major law firm, but it's even more difficult for those with kids. The old boys' club thinks kids severely cramp your working style and availability. Same thing at Morgan. I see it all the time. Capable women are passed over because management thinks they will be less effective at their job because they are mothers. They think it will get in the way." Blake sighed, "Look, Babe, this is your big chance—take it. I'll stay home with Cooper."

"No way! This is your big day too. I know how long you've worked on this IPO; today is your day to shine. You can't stay home." Amy said but didn't believe: "I'll always be able to get another interview."

"Maybe, Amy, but you've also worked hard for this opportunity. If you don't show, they will probably give the job to the other guy. No, I'll stay with Coop."

The couple looked at each other and laughed. Each cared so much for the other that they were willing to sacrifice significantly to make the other happy.

Amy and Blake were both steadfast in their decision until Blake came up with an idea.

"Let's flip."

"Flip?"

"Flip a coin. The winner goes, and the loser stays home. What do you say?"

"I say, you go, and I stay home; forget the flip."

Blake loved that Amy always took the high road when push came to shove. "No, the deal is we flip, or both of us will stay home."

Blake pulled a quarter out of the pocket of his new suit and showed it to her in his palm. "Winner calls it."

"No, I'm not calling; I'm staying with Coop."

"Well, if you won't call, I'll call for you, so what will it be. Heads or tails?

Reluctantly, Amy called, "Tails."

Blake tossed it up. The coin fell to the hardwood floor and spun around, wobbling to a stop: "Tails, you win." Before Amy could argue, Blake was out of his suit, running around in his briefs, looking for his sweatpants.

*****

Blake silently groaned, rolled over, and covered his head. He wondered how you un-remember a morning that proved pivotal for him and the rest of his life … Cooper's too. He would never forget his Amy and the oh-so-short time they had together. He had met her while at Princeton, and she was a junior at Bryn Mawr College, some fifty miles from Princeton. She was a "Jersey Girl," but not the rock and roll kind. Her family was from Cherry Hill; like Blake, she was an only child. Amy was part of the Bryn Mawr choir, and the group traveled around the Ivy League performing intercollegiate women's concerts. His fellow Princetonians always said the concerts were a ruse that allowed girls to meet the Ivy Leaguers. Blake thought that typical of the egocentric student-elites who thought God took cues from them—thankfully, he was not like them.

Blake put his hands behind his head and adjusted his pillow. He loved these moments, the happy memories when he remembered Amy and their time together. He smiled when he recalled the first time he saw her. She had come to Princeton for a concert and to see a boy she was dating, some rich kid from the city. But when he saw them together at a fraternity party, he knew instinctively they were not a match. She was beautiful, refined, and preppy, and her date was a New York show-off in his Alfa Romeo convertible, fancy too-tight jeans, expensive sneakers, flashing around Daddy's Amex card.

Amy, the thought of her, made him smile. So pretty and friendly too. She had sun-kissed, highlighted auburn hair, which she brushed back from her face when she walked.

The sun was peeking through the torn shade on the window as he had his last recollection. Amy had dropped the New York boyfriend but still performed at the concerts, and they met one weekend at a Sigma party—introduced by Stu, who knew everyone. He wanted the memory to stop there. But he knew it wouldn't.

*****

That morning Amy caught the subway downtown, and Blake prepared to spend the day taking care of Cooper. He figured he'd send out for some soup at lunchtime. It would be good for

Cooper's stomach. Cooper remained in bed, and Blake took a rare opportunity to read the morning paper and enjoy a cup of homebrewed coffee from their newly acquired expresso machine.

The phone rang just after 9:30. It was one of the traders at Morgan who knew Blake wasn't coming in that day. Blake heard the panic in the guy's voice.

"Hey Blake, turn on the TV!"

"What?" Blake asked. "What are you talking about, and why are you screaming?" Blake could hear commotion in the background.

"Turn it on, Blake, any channel, just turn it on. You're not going to believe it. The market is going to go ballistic. It's the World Trade Center. Some asshole hit it with a plane!"

It took less than a nanosecond for Blake to put this together. The tall tower on the East River was on fire, and on the eighty-ninth floor of that tower was Drinker Biddle & Reath, his wife's firm.

On Tuesday, at 9:46 A.M., Blake's life changed when American Airlines Flight 11 slammed into the North Tower. It changed not only for him but for his precious son, now motherless.

Blake could barely function after Amy's tragic death. He had profound guilt that Amy would be alive except for a lousy quarter. Gnawing, endless grief consumed him. He couldn't sleep without her next to him. He refused to wash her pillowcase because he was convinced it still smelled of her botanical-scented, expensive shampoo, with notes of peppermint and honey. For a long time, an hour could not pass without Blake feeling the sting of loneliness and despair. Cooper seemed numb for weeks but miraculously made a sort of peace with the loss by talking to his mother's photograph.

So much had to change after that moment in time. Blake knew he could not continue the rat race and long hours at JP Morgan while raising Cooper properly, and to be honest, the fire in the belly that a trader needed to be effective seemed to have flickered out. He realized he had to make some profound changes, so he resigned from Morgan. After a while, Blake knew he had to find a way to support himself and Cooper, so he made some calls.

"Good morning, Stu; it's Blake Anderson. How the hell are you?"

"Good, buddy, and you?" Stu immediately regretted the question. He knew Blake couldn't possibly be well after what happened to Amy and his sudden departure from JP Morgan.

"I'm hanging in there. Thanks for asking. And how about you, Debbie, and the kids?"

Stu was Blake's fraternity brother at Princeton. They were close through school after an almost-inhuman pledging of Sigma Alpha Theta. That kind of experience created lifelong bonds, nothing not exposed for the others to see and nothing more important than joint survival of the barbaric rituals of Sigma Alpha Theta. Stu was from New York City and had a triple alumni family. His great-grandfather, grandfather, and father were all Princeton and Sigmas too. Only about 15 percent of the student body belonged to fraternities, but Stu had no choice given his legacy. As for Blake, Stu's roommate, he went along for the ride. They were from different worlds. Blake was from Missouri and on a full baseball scholarship. As Blake put it, Stu was a fourth-generation Princetonian who spent his family money faster than the mint could print.

"Stu, I was wondering if you could do me a favor. I hate to ask, but I want to keep Cooper at St. Tim's, but the tuition is way more than I can pay. I have a part-time job, but it hardly keeps us in beans. So, I know you are on the board at St. Tim's, and I wondered if you would help me get a teaching job there. I understand that the children of teachers get free tuition, which would allow Cooper to stay put."

"Teaching? You want to give up Wall Street? Bro, that's where the big bucks are. Are you nuts?"

"I' m just not ready to go back into the Wall Street grind. In fact, I am pretty sure I never will be. After Amy." Blake paused and welled up. "I had to rethink a lot about life. It's taken a while, but I need to get back to work, just not something that is so consuming and that would keep me away from Cooper."

Stu listened but did not speak.

"But teaching might be something I could get into. I majored in education, so I'm pretty sure I'd meet any school's requirements."

"Yeah, I remember you majored in education, and you remember how I told you teaching was for losers and that the money was on Wall Street. And how after graduation, I introduced you to the guys at Morgan, and they loved you." Stu bit his tongue and immediately regretted the reference to "loser," given that Blake was now seriously considering teaching.

"I remember it well. Especially those grueling SEC tests required to get my broker's licenses."

"And you passed them with nearly perfect scores! Unlike me, who had to take them twice."

"Twice? As I recall, you took the Series 7 three times."

"OK, OK, don't rub it in." Stu could tell by Blake's voice that he was serious about teaching. "Look, Blake, I can't promise anything, but if you are really serious about teaching at St. Tim's I can look into it and use some influence if necessary. Having a Princeton man on the faculty wouldn't hurt the school's credentials. Parents love that kind of stuff. I know you'd be a great teacher, but I still think you should stick it out on The Street."

"Not for me anymore, Stu. I'm done with that rat race, and besides, I want to be near Cooper, he needs me a lot more than some billionaire peddling his IPO."

Stu continued, "You know, even at schools, money talks. My dad and mom built St. Tim's new chapel. So maybe some room can be made for a smart guy like you if I asked. Let me check it out, and I'll get back to you."

Stu remembered a night at Princeton when he was just a sophomore. He and Blake were at an out-of-bounds bar. He was as drunk as a skunk and made the mistake of trying to pick up some local honey. The girl was some farm boy's sister—a farm boy as big as a New York Giants linebacker. The farm boy didn't take kindly to the advances and was about to pound Stu into oblivion. Blake saw what was about to happen and pulled the chair out from under the townie, allowing them an opportunity to run the hell out of the bar. A few weeks later, that very townie's picture was in the local paper for being arrested on assault charges for beating someone unconscious. After that, Blake was Stu's wingman.

"Thanks, pal. Anything you can do will be appreciated, and I'll owe you."

"Don't thank me yet. If anyone owes, it's me. Be well, brother."

It took three interviews and a day of substituting before Blake got the job. No question Stu had a lot to do with it, and Blake was grateful to be able to keep Cooper in the school he loved, with free tuition.

*****

Blake stumbled out of bed, tripping on the bunched-up shirts and pants Cooper had piled up for him to take to the laundromat. "Nice going, Cooper," he mumbled. "Coffee, I need coffee."

This apartment was also a recent change. When he left Morgan, he and Cooper moved out of their duplex on the park. Now settled in a cozy, code for tiny, walk-up apartment, the dynamic duo lived unencumbered by long-gone amenities, like a washer and dryer stacked discreetly in the kitchen behind attractive cabinetry and a doorman to take residents' clothes to the cleaners. He reasoned that the step down was temporary since there was talk of insurance settlements and government grants to families of 911 survivors. But he knew you couldn't pay bills with talk, and even if they got the money, it would be tainted, and he would have a hard time using it. Blake hated the thought of some bureaucrat or personal injury lawyers weighing the amount they would give. How much was Amy Anderson's life worth? To them, some number, but to him and Cooper, no amount. He'd already decided anything they received would go into a trust for Cooper. Blake would continue living very modestly.

The coffee maker sputtered and steamed as his last K-cup produced the deep dark cup of donut shop brew. Gone were the days of the five-dollar Starbucks. *Black it is,* he thought. Ran out of milk the day before yesterday.

On the surface, this existence was a comedown. But the reality was that his relationship and closeness to Cooper had never been better. And that, he knew this was far better than having an army of doormen and the biggest meanest Maytag that money could buy.

Cooper barreled into the kitchen. "Dad, let's go play catch. It's going to be nice."

"Nice? It's pretty windy, and it looks like it's going to rain. That's not nice."

"Not that kind of nice, Dad, the kind of nice like when you and I play catch. The weather doesn't matter. Come on, get dressed...."

Blake could not resist his little man, so he grabbed and squeezed him into his arms and thought: *This kid is my world. He has a heart of an angel and looks like one too!*

One of the strongest bonds that Blake and Cooper shared was baseball. As a boy, from the earliest age, Blake and his own dad lived and breathed the game. He collected baseball cards and watched every game he could. Where he grew up, Missouri produced its fair share of major leaguers, and Blake prayed to be one of them. He had been captain of his high school team and was recruited by Princeton with a full scholarship for his talent and academic excellence. Coming from Missouri, he had little exposure to the "big time," so it was education that he chose as a major. He thought teaching was a noble profession, allowing him to stay in touch with both kids and baseball.

Blake was a cookie-cutter of an All-American; he was tall, handsome, wicked smart, and played baseball like Mickey Mantle. There was talk of Major League drafting and the potential for a seven-figure salary. When he sustained an injury to his pitching arm, it meant the MLB was no longer in the cards. But no matter, Blake passed on his love for the game to Cooper. The kid was destined to love it. Despite Amy's preference for Eric, the very name Cooper was agreed upon because it was reminiscent of where baseball's Hall of Fame resided: Cooperstown, New York.

Every waking moment Blake and Cooper talked baseball. Who struck out, who walked, and who was a "bum." Blake had access to the company box at Yankee Stadium when he was at Morgan. Most traders would rather drink or golf than watch baseball, allowing Cooper and him endless opportunities to fill the often-empty VIP seats. Blake would take Cooper to the memorabilia shop in Brooklyn and buy baseball cards every Sunday night. Cooper loved the cards and the experience of talking baseball with the owner and his customers, all of whom fell in love with the little man. Last, he loved the bubble gum with every pack of collectibles.

"Hold on, big guy," Blake called out. "We got some chores to do. First, we have to clean up this place. I know we are sloppy during the week, but Saturday is clean-up day. Then we have to go to the laundromat."

"Dad, not the laundromat! That's so boring."

"Well, what would you rather be, bored or smelly?

"I don't know. Bobby Richards in my class is smelly, and kids like him."

"Yeah, But Bobby Richards isn't you; you have a father who doesn't like smelly kids."

"OK, I'll go, but let's bring the baseball almanac to play trivia while we wait for that yucky dryer."

"It's a deal. Now eat some Cheerios and brush your teeth; the dryer awaits."

The boys made their way to the apartment door, and Cooper hesitated.

"Wait, Dad, I forgot to kiss Mom goodbye!" He picked up the silver-framed picture of Amy and tenderly kissed her photograph on the cheek. "Goodbye, Mommy. I love you in heaven."

CHAPTER TWO
A Big Choice

Blake's job at St. Timothy's was satisfying. He taught math and coached boys' baseball. On the surface, things were copacetic. He loved the faculty and getting to teach and mentor the kids brought joy to his life—it helped him breathe when most days memories of Amy stabbed at his heart. He particularly related to the parents, being one himself. And coaching baseball was his fantasy come true.

It didn't take long before he became one of the most popular members of the St. Tim's staff. Even Alice, the sour old school nurse, smiled broadly when Blake walked by.

Blake often shared his thoughts and observations with the other teachers in the teachers' lounge. He had become friendly with several of them and especially enjoyed talking with Sam Longworth, the science teacher and fellow baseball enthusiast.

"Sam, did you see the game last night?"

"Hell yeah, and I think the umpire was blind when he called Mendoza out. That was definitely a ball. Totally outside."

"It was close, and the crowd didn't like the call, that's for sure."

"Hey Blake, I hear that Mrs. Blackmer told Angie, the school secretary, that she's going to retire at the end of the term. You know what that means: vice principal's job will be open."

"Really, Angie told you that?"

"Well, not exactly. She told Nick, the janitor, who told Nurse Alice, who told me.... But confidentially."

"Quite the chain of communications, I'd say."

"Well, Angie is a reliable source since her ears are bigger than her....well, they're pretty big. She sits right outside McHenry's office and usually gets it right."

McHenry... the principal from hell! Since Blake started, he felt Mr. McHenry had it in for him. But he couldn't quite figure out why. Sam did tell Blake point-blank why, but it seemed inconceivable to him. How could Mr. McHenry be jealous of him? For God's sake, he was a widower with a son to raise on his own.

"Hey Blake, maybe you should interview for vice-principal. You got such a rapport with the kids, the parents love you, and the way you took hold of the fundraising, you'd be a perfect choice."

"Well, not so fast, Sam. I'm here to teach, and that's perfectly fine with me."

"Maybe, but the word around is that there is no better choice."

The apartment's phone rang about a week later. Cooper was already sleeping, and Blake was correcting papers on the tiny dining room table. The dim light from the small chandelier was hardly bright enough to see. Three of the five bulbs were out, and Blake had it on his list to get some new ones the next payday.

"Hello."

"Hi Blake, it's Stu. Is this a bad time?"

"No, Stu, it's not. It's never a bad time for you. What's up?"

"So, you know that Blackmer is retiring at the end of the year."

"Yeah, apparently that word has been out for some time. The gossip mills at school's been grinding overtime."

"There was a meeting last night, and the board has picked me to head up the search committee for Blackmer's replacement. The choice has to be the right one since ultimately the person could succeed Mr. McHenry."

Blake thought that would be a wonderful thing. McHenry was his nemesis. "Sounds like a real challenge." Blake knew working for McHenry wasn't a dream job, and a new vice-principal would have it rough being underfoot continually. McHenry didn't seem the type to mentor or take anyone under his wing.

"Yeah. It will be. But a funny thing happened at the meeting."

"Really, what?"

"The board chairwoman asked the members if they had any suggestions for anyone they thought would make a good candidate for the job. If they did, she asked them to formally submit them in writing for consideration."

"So, what's so funny about that?"

"Five members had no suggestions, and four members independently submitted your name."

"My name? Are you serious?"

"Yes, I'm serious. The chairwoman asked me, as head of the search committee, to approach you on the QT to see if there was any interest. If there was, it could save a lot of time looking outside. You see, everyone loves that Princeton credential, along with the bang-up job you've done with the fundraising, and the fact that you are a known entity...well, it seems like a perfect fit."

Blake exhaled into the phone and continued to listen.

"Oh, yeah, Blake. Get this, and don't let it go to your head, but two board members thought you are so cute and had an irresistible personality."

"Is this high school? Come on, Stu. Not funny."

"Maybe not funny. But being great-looking didn't hurt you. Those Park Avenue housewives like you, and that makes a difference."

Blake grimaced into the phone and continued to hear Stu out.

"But, back to business. Blake, before we spin our wheels, the board wants to know if you would seriously consider taking the vice-principal's office. It would mean a modest pay increase and a great credential on your curriculum vitae."

"I don't think so, Stu. I'm just a neophyte in education, and besides, McHenry hates me."

"Don't worry about not having years of experience. You have all that it takes; smarts proved by that Princeton degree, administrative skills, majored in education, and a winning way with people, particularly with board members."

Blake listened. and his mind raced.

"Look, Blake, this is a great opportunity, so don't just pass on it without serious consideration."

"I don't know. Maybe it would be good for Cooper to see his dad succeed. Kind of a good example. Especially after all we've been through and how depressed we've both been. I want him to see me being happy again."

"Right, a good example. So, what say you?"

"Let me sleep on it. But one thing is for sure; I'm not giving up my job at the memorabilia shop. Cooper loves it there, and Mr. Como, the owner, would be heartbroken."

"Who says you can't do both? Let's talk in the morning. Ciao."

He finished correcting the math papers and sat on the old settee in front of the TV, which he bought just before he quit his job at Morgan. Money back then was fast in coming and fast in going out. A young family living in New York was an expensive ordeal, and saving was just beginning to have value. When Blake left Morgan, it didn't take long to go through what little they had put aside. Cooper and he moved from the posh duplex on the park to a third-floor walk-up, learning frugality along the way. Amy and he had rented a furnished apartment, so when he moved there was little to bring. The fact was that he didn't have much, and life was going to be a lot different. He knew there would likely be some kind of settlement money for 911 victims' families, but Blake didn't even like thinking about that. Besides, he wanted that set aside for Cooper. They would be fine with their new lifestyle. The call from Stu was thought-provoking. He wondered if taking the board up on their offer was the right move. It had so many implications. For one, it meant making a career commitment to education. Was he ready to toss his Wall Street career once and for all? Another consideration was the hours. He knew for sure that doing the kind of job that was needed would require more hours at school, and how would that affect Cooper and their time together? Then there was Mr. Como's shop. He really loved that job, and the customers were so kind to him and Cooper. And lastly, Blake needed to address his relationship with Mr. McHenry. There wasn't good chemistry between them, and should he become vice principal, he would have to work directly under the man. McHenry's reputation for compromises was notorious: he never made them.

He pondered: St. Tim's was a great place to teach. The kids were eager to learn, and the parents were involved in every aspect of the school. He often would chat with his fellow teachers in the lounge, comparing notes on the students and sharing insights.

Blake decided to call it a night, but it turned out to be a long one filled with tossing, turning, and sleeplessness.

At St. Tim's, like most institutions, there were no secrets. Blake arrived early the following day with his decision still unmade. He walked through the center hall, and a couple of the other instructors greeted him and quickly disappeared, whispering to one another. The school nurse came out of her office, took one look at Blake, and did a 360 back into her room. Blake stepped into the secretary's office to pick up his daily notices and mail.

"Good morning, Angie. That color looks lovely on you. You look so nice."

"Thank you, Mr. Anderson, and so do you....Very nice." Angie wasn't kidding. Blake always looked great. His tall, fit stature was perfect for the two-thousand-dollar custom-made suits he had acquired in his long-gone, high-flying trading days. He had a generous crop of dirty blond hair, which he kept styled like a youthful schoolboy.

"So, Angie, what's new?"

"What's new? Mr. Anderson, well, I'm sure you are the one who would know best."

"What do you mean...?"

Angie smiled broadly and stuck her head inside a file drawer, ending the conversation.

As he exited the office, Blake ran smack into Mr. McHenry, who was just arriving for the day.

"Good morning, Sir. How are you this fine morning?"

Mr. McHenry looked at Blake and gave a grim smile and a curt nod as he hurried past him. While McHenry was effusively nice to parents, to the teachers he was ... well, McHenry. And to Blake he was the most McHenry-ish of all.

Lunch break came, and Blake pulled up a chair in the teacher's lounge and opened his brown bag filled with the previous night's leftovers. He picked out a napkin and then an apple, which sat on top of a Tupperware container filled with something brownish. Then he remembered—curried pork. He recalled lunch at JP Morgan when management would have lavishly catered buffets set up in the office so that the traders would not waste any time going to restaurants. Lobster salad, chafing dishes with a hot entrée to die for, fresh fruit, and for the "diet be damned" bunch, hot pastrami and corn beef sandwiches with heaps of savory mustard or Thousand Island dressing. A three-tiered silver tray with sweets from Lorraine's, the hottest bakery downtown, topped off the spread.

Blake's lunchtime flashback was interrupted when Sam pulled up the chair next to him. He gave Blake a soft punch on the arm and said: "You dog, you."

"Dog, what the hell are you talking about?"

"Come on, Blakey-boy, you know."

"No, I don't. Give me a break. You and everyone else this morning are acting really weird. Like they know something I don't."

"Come on, man. I'm your buddy, don't mess with me. Give me the scoop."

Sam wondered if Blake was being coy or if he just didn't know. "Blake, the word is out, so give it up."

Blake gave Sam a blank look.

"Well, everyone is talking. Like I said, the word is out."

"Out? Come on, level with me."

"The word, Blake, is that you are only an announcement memo away from being vice-principal."

"What! That's not true." He lowered his voice to a whisper. "You're kidding, right?"

Sam looked directly into Blake's eyes, and Blake realized he was being honest. "You don't know, do you?"

"No. What?"

"Well, according to Nick, the janitor, who heard it from the nurse, who was told by Angie, who took notes at the board meeting the other night, you are the pick for the job...vice-principal

Blake felt like they were playing the telephone game when one person tells the next, and that person passes it on to the next, and in the end, the original message is completely changed.

"Sam, let me level with you. I have not been given the job. A board member called last night to feel me out to see if I might be interested. I didn't answer because I wanted to think about it. So, everyone has jumped to conclusions based on hearsay and unsubstantiated gossip."

Sam leaned in. "So, it's true; you will be the VP."

"That's not what I said, for crying out loud. I said I was thinking about it, that's all."

Sam stuck out his hand. "Shake, buddy, or should I say Mr. Vice Principal? It's nice to know people in high places! Congratulations."

"You're hopeless, Sam, hopeless."

CHAPTER THREE
ON ONE CONDITION

IN ADDITION TO STU, APPARENTLY TWO PARENTS ON THE BOARD really championed him. He had helped diagnose Mrs. Rockwood's son's dyslexia—and had helped Charlie's self-esteem. Jack Mallory loved the way Blake could fundraise—not to mention the afterschool math club he had started. Jack Mallory was worth fifty million dollars. And he was also passionate about the school. Lucy Littleton, an alumna and influential member, fell in love with Blake from the first, as did the whole board. Everyone could see Blake was exceptional with young people.

Blake decided to take the job. It was a difficult decision because he had real trepidations. Not about doing the job or being competent. He knew his skills, and what he lacked in experience, he made up for with common sense gained mainly by being a good father and accomplished businessman. What troubled him was the already rocky relationship he had with Mr. McHenry. Blake later learned that McHenry called six board members urging them to vote against Blake and sent a memo to the board chairman with a veiled threat that he would resign should the appointment be approved. Despite that, the board voted unanimously in favor. Almost immediately after the approval McHenry launched his campaign to discredit Blake.

On the first Friday of the month, St. Tim's had an open house. Blake and the rest of the staff welcomed parents, grandparents, and other guests.

"Good afternoon, Mr. Anderson," gushed the recent widow, Kathrine Del Monte. "I can't tell you how happy I am that our new vice principal is you. You will do a splendid job, I'm sure."

Kathrine was a bit older than Blake, and since her wealthy husband passed, she had more than ample amounts of plastic surgery, so much that her original face seemed a distant memory. When the term started, and she showed up with her two less-than-charming kids, the staff didn't recognize her.

"Thank you, Mrs. Del Monte. I appreciate your confidence. It means a lot to me."

Kathrine looked Blake over like one might examine a prime rib they were contemplating buying for a dinner party. She thought, *He's a keeper, and in that suit, he looks like a million bucks, and out of it, probably, two million!"* Her mind continued ... and wouldn't he'd fit right in at the club? She could see him on her arm already, or better yet, waking up next to her at her villa in Sardinia, next season.

The club was the Gotham Club, New York's most elite social venue. Her husband had been on the board there, and since her "widowism," she always felt awkward attending the galas alone. Sure, she knew that many of the "old blue blood dames" who lost their husbands, some of them decades ago, came to the parties with a hired escort. Not the sleazy kind you hear about in the gossip rags, but men ranging from their thirties well into their sixties. They came from very diverse backgrounds: eye candy dance instructors, personal trainers, and the like. Others just ne'er-do-well gents or metrosexual gigolos who loved to dress up and be seen. All of them lived precariously through rich women. Nothing was expected from then other than looking marvelous and dancing like Fred Astaire. It was unspoken, but sex was totally out of the question for both the escorts and the grand ladies.

A kind of competition developed over the years among the widows and divorcees as to who could bring the most attractive fellow. Often, more than usually, the men, particularly the younger ones, were considerably prettier than their hostesses who hid behind remarkably similar-looking faces created by New York's best plastic surgeons, hundreds of karats of jewels, and hideously expensive Bergdorf's and Chanel originals designed for beautiful bodies that they did not possess.

"So, Mr. Anderson, I understand that you live alone with your darling little boy, hm...what's his name? Topper, isn't it? My kids just love him to death."

"No, his name is Cooper."

"Cooper, of course, he's the adorable little redhead with the Mohawk haircut and sad face."

"He's blond, and I like to think he is quite happy, smiling much of the time."

"Oh, yes, the blond, the petite little blond boy, just so sweet, I know he'll sprout up someday, don't you worry."

Cooper wasn't by any measure petite, but Blake decided to give up correcting this bizarre-looking woman with fire engine–red lips the size of pin cushions. He thought maybe she got them caught somewhere and they were swollen.

Blake knew who the Del Monte kids were—all the faculty did. They were among the most unruly and spoiled ones in the school. The boys were in his class and had a reputation for lying.

"Oh, I know both of them, and they are real individualists." That was Blake's code word for selfish and obnoxious brats.

"Well, Blake ... may I call you Blake?" Kathrine continued, not waiting for an answer. "I know you are running the fundraising efforts here at St. Tim's, and I have a marvelous, more than a marvelous idea to help the school make oodles!" She paused, puckered up her lips and put her little finger to them and smoothed her lipstick.

"Mrs. Del Monte ..."

"It's Kathrine, darling, I told you that already, Kathrine."

As tempting as it might have been, Blake decided to pass on putting this woman in her place since it was probably politically unwise. "Anything anyone can do to help St. Tim's is always welcome."

"Marvelous, darling. I knew you'd be all hands on board." Kathrine secretly wished "all hands on me." "So, here's my fabulous idea. You see, the club, you know the Gotham Club, has an Oktoberfest Ball, and I thought I could get the club to donate, say, forty or fifty tickets to the school, and we could auction them off. Most people would pay a fortune to get their nose into a place like the Gotham Club. It's very restricted, you know, mostly limited to the 400 crowd."

Blake, coming from Missouri, really didn't know or understand the New York social scene but recalled reading about the New York 400 in *A Night to Remember*, the story of the *Titanic*. He read people like the Astors and Rockefellers were all part of that bunch … tycoons and captains of industry, wealthy beyond imagination. "Your idea, Mrs. Del Monte, is a good one. Let me run it by Mr. McHenry and Mrs. Brady, head of the parents' association."

"Mrs. Brady, really? Don't bother. She wouldn't have the slightest idea about how valuable such access is since …" Kathrine hesitated to find the right words, and finally, the wrong ones slipped out. "People like the Bradys are not in the same category as …. well, they're new money, you know." Realizing how unfiltered her words came out, she ended midsentence. "You'll see, darling. Everyone will love it."

What Blake didn't know was that Kathrine had a master plan. This was her way of getting Blake to be her escort and introduce him to her friends. After that, she assumed, he'd get a good taste of the kind of social life he could have with her, and she'd own him, just like that gorgeous pair of Jimmy Choo's she just bought. He'd be putty in her well-manicured, diamond-festooned hands. Kathrine grabbed Blake's elbow and drew him closer. "Just take it from me. It's a great idea, McHenry and Brady will do exactly as I say."

*****

Kathrine's idea turned out to be a pretty good one. However, the club only donated two tables of ten guests each to be auctioned off. The bidding for the first table was robust, and Kathrine aggressively increased the bid each time someone raised their numbered paddle.

"Do I hear $3,500?" Asked the auctioneer on loan from Sotheby's…another string pulled by Kathrine.

"$3,500," called out Dr. Longmire.

"$4,000!" countered, Kathrine.

"$4,500," shouted another parent sitting in the back row, now furiously waving her paddle.

Kathrine decided to end things. She held her paddle high and offered her bid: "$10,000."

The room fell silent, and all eyes turned toward Kathrine. The auctioneer asked, "Are you certain madame, $10,000?"

Kathrine looked over at Mr. McHenry and then at Blake. "Yes, but there is one condition."

"Condition? That is most unusual to have a condition."

"Well, Sir, my condition is something that will cost the school nothing and close the deal on my bid, assuming Mr. McHenry agrees."

McHenry stood up and waited to hear the condition.

"My condition is that I get to choose a faculty member to be my companion for the ball. What do you say, Mr. McHenry, do I get to pick someone?

McHenry knew a $10,000 donation didn't drop out of the sky every day. "Of course, Mrs. Del Monte, the school would be more than happy to accommodate that condition."

"Fabulous. My choice for the ball is Mr. Blake Anderson."

Blake's face turned white. *Oh my God,* he thought. *Captain Ahab has harpooned me.*

"$10,000! Sold!" shouted out the auctioneer. "Table for ten at the Gotham Club's Oktoberfest along with Mr. Anderson for the night."

The crowd cheered and laughed all at the same time, and Sam later swore to Blake that he saw Mrs. Del Monte actually licking her ballooned lips.

CHAPTER FOUR
Could It Get Any Worse?

A note peeked out of Blake's cubby in the front office. It would be the first of many to follow. He picked it up and began to read.

Mr. Anderson,

Effective immediately:

I am directing you to head up the extra-help program held each morning from 6:45 AM until classes begin at approximately 8:15 AM. You will have to monitor all tutoring programs, enforce school rules, especially those relating to uniform compliance, and make weekly status reports, in duplicate, directly to me.

A week later, another note appeared.

Mr. Anderson,

I understand that the milk being served in our cafeteria is frequently spoiled. I would like you to contact the supplier, advise him of the issue, and check to see that the temperature in the refrigerated units is correct. If the students or faculty report spoiled milk, I would like you to confiscate unfinished containers, store them in the refrigerator and return them to the vendor the next day for credit. Careful accounting of how many containers were returned must be made so we can ensure receiving proper credit.

Several other directives appeared in the weeks to come, But the one that outraged Blake the most came on Friday morning, addressed to the entire faculty and staff. Blake thought it couldn't get worse than this.

To: All Team Members:

Several parents have brought to my attention that their children found the restrooms to be unpleasant. This must not stand. Mr. Nick, our janitor, tells me he is far too stretched to handle this problem. Therefore, I am assigning Mr. Anderson the responsibility of implementing a solution. Twice a day, he will inspect all of the restrooms. Those that may have offensive or excessive odors will be treated. This will require working with a plumber as well as placing fragrant room deodorants strategically in the restrooms. To determine popular opinion on the most preferred, Mr. Anderson will obtain samples of various restroom deodorants and have them available for a staff "scent test." Based on the survey results, Mr. Anderson will provide a written report for this office's review. Once the most desirable scent is determined, Mr. Anderson will implement a program to place said deodorants. In addition, Mr. Anderson shall conduct mini-seminars for the students emphasizing the need for hygiene in the toilet and the importance of proper flushing. I have designated this program: "Operation Clean Flush." I urge all of you to cooperate with Mr. Anderson, our new Toilet Czar.

Mr. McHenry, Principal

Blake knew that McHenry was just trying to unnerve him, hoping that he would lose his cool and do something that would cause him a problem. Blake wouldn't take the bait. Despite the mocking by some of the older kids who would whisper "woosh" whenever Blake entered the room, he concentrated on teaching, coaching, and raising money, lots of money, for the school.

Cooper was thrilled that he made the baseball team and over the moon when his team members voted him in as captain and later starting pitcher, which was, in his opinion, the best and most important position. Blake assured Cooper that the choice was the team's and not his as the coach.

On the way home from school, Cooper was bursting with pride and nervousness.

"Dad," Cooper quietly said. "Do you think I'll screw it up?"

"What?"

"Pitching on the team. I mean, it's the most important position and, you know, just getting started, I might ..."

"Just getting started? I don't think so. You and I have been playing ball ever since you were able to walk. And you have one of the strongest pitching arms for a guy your age."

"You're just saying that because you're my dad."

"Well, not just because of that, but because I'm the coach too. Coaches know talent and potential when they see it. And, my little man, you got both."

Cooper leaned over and punched his dad's arm, a loving punch. "You're the best!"

The dynamic duo road the long subway ride from midtown chic to Brooklyn grunge in relative silence. Cooper basked in the glory of his newfound position, and Blake thought back to when he was a boy in Missouri with his dad.

From his earliest recollection, Blake wanted to be a professional baseball player. He was a die-hard Royals fan but secretly loved the New York Yankees. He always thought of that team as "big time," and that's what he wanted to be someday. But living in Missouri, it wasn't the most popular thing to support any team other than the Royals.

Every night, he and his father would do what his dad called "Baseball and Grown-up Talk." One particular conversation came to mind as the train sped towards the Brooklyn Bridge en route to their apartment.

*****

"Hey, Bud." That was Danny Anderson's pet name for Blake. The two were lobbing their 400ish pitch of the day. By the time Blake was fourteen, he and his dad must have passed that ball back and forth a million times.

"Yeah, Dad?"

"You know, people should always think before they speak."

"What? Why are you even saying that?"

"Oh, I don't know, but as you get older, it's important to measure your words."

"Measure my words? What? With a ruler?"

"No." His dad laughed. "Measure your words means thinking about what you will say before you do."

"Why?"

"Well, suppose I didn't like Mom's pot roast tonight."

"Yeah, but it was delicious."

"I know, but suppose I didn't like it, and I said, 'This is awful, and I hate it.' How do you think that would make mom feel?"

"Not good. She worked hard to make it. My friends think she is the best cook out of all the moms. And dads. Mr. Levinson does all the cooking in Marc's house."

"Exactly. Remarks like that are hurtful and unkind. So, as I said, measure your words, and sometimes it's better to keep things to yourself.'

"I see. Like when I told Ronnie I thought he stunk at baseball, and he quit."

"Yes, that's exactly what I mean. And how do you think that made Ronnie feel?"

"Not so good, I guess." Blake stopped pitching for a minute and looked down at his well-worn glove. "Dad, do you think it's too late to apologize to him?"

"No, Buddy, it's never too late to apologize."

"Good, I'm going to. And I'm going to ask him to play catch with us, and maybe he'll get better."

"That's my man."

*****

It was through moments like those and hundreds of others that Blake learned so much. He learned not only how to be a grown-up but also what it is to be a man, what sportsmanship means, and how important it is to be honest yet kind at the same time.

The subway was almost at their stop when Blake had another fond recollection. It was the day he received the letter from Princeton's baseball coach offering him a full scholarship, perhaps the happiest day in his life, only behind his wedding day to Amy and Cooper's birth.

"Open it," demanded Blake's dad. "Open it."

"I can't! I'm terrified it will be a rejection."

Danny Anderson sat his son down and said: "Blake, life is full of surprises, good and bad, and men have to take bad news along with good news. Whatever it is, it is. So, open the envelope and remember this. You are a great, no … incredible ballplayer, and an even better person, if they haven't figured it out, then shame on them."

Blake looked his father straight in the eye. He knew, his dad always told it like it was. Without further hesitation, Blake carefully opened the envelope with the prestigious Princeton crest on the return address. He read the first paragraph, and tears came to his eyes.

"Here, Dad, you read it."

> *Dear Blake,*
>
> *It is a great pleasure that I offer you Princeton's Mandel four-year full scholarship for excellence in baseball. …*

Blake's dad paused and looked up. "You did it, Bud. You did it!"

*****

The subway was making the final bend just before their stop when Blake remembered another moment. It was years after he graduated Princeton cum laude and when he was going through his father's things after his death. He found a yellowed envelope. Blake recognized it immediately. It was the acceptance letter from Princeton that his dad had kept all this time. He opened it and found the original document, along with a small card, the kind they hand out at Sunday school. It was a little prayer that ended in: *Thank you, Lord, for these thy gifts that we have received, from thy bounty.* Under the prayer was his father's handwritten notation. "Forever grateful, dear God, thank you for blessing my boy."

Blake fought the lump in his throat and pulled himself together. Cooper jumped to his feet as the train slowed to a stop. "Come on, Dad. I'm starving."

CHAPTER FIVE
THE CITY OF LOVE

DINNERTIME WAS ALWAYS THE HARDEST FOR BLAKE. COOKING was not among his expertise, and doing dishes afterward was drudgery; the days of the dishwasher were long gone.

"What's for dinner, Dad?"

Pretending to be a big shot chef, he replied in his pitiful French. "Chef Blake has something extraordinary for you, Monsieur Cooper. It's today's special: Doigts de poulet avec frites français et."

French, he thought. It was the language he and Amy were trying to learn in preparation for their trip to Paris. Blake had won the trip for being the biggest producer in the New York office for two months running.

He remembered how excited Amy was when he broke the news.

*****

"What did you say?" Amy screamed. "Paris?"

"Yes, Babe, Paris. All expenses paid. Trip for two, but we'll add Cooper and make it for three."

"Oh my God, when is this trip?"

"Whenever we like. We are free to book it at our convenience."

"Great!" Amy, the consummate planner, began: "We'll do it right after school is finished. And that will give us plenty of time to learn French."

"French? Are you kidding? I'm terrible at languages."

"Oh, come on, Blake, it will be fun. We can take the course together, at Berlitz. Maybe we could get a two-for-one deal?"

Blake knew there was no point in arguing. Once Amy made up her mind, the die was cast. And anyway, it probably would be fun to learn French. You never knew when it would come in handy again. There was always Morgan's Paris office.

"OK, but on one condition."

"And that is?"

Blake leaned over and whispered in Amy's ear.

"You dirty old man. If you don't mind, I'll stick to American kissing."

The trip was fantastic. Amy dragged poor Cooper and him to every tourist sight in Paris. Each night the threesome would stroll the Champs-Elysees and take hundreds of pictures. Cooper was disappointed to learn that baseball was of little significance in France and that practically no one ever heard of it.

"We'd have to go to Tokyo for that, Coop," Blake said.

So, Cooper concentrated on reading the Baseball Almanac and playing catch in the hotel hallway with his dad.

The accommodations were perfect; a two-room suite with a bedroom and sitting room where Cooper slept on a fold-down cot. For Amy and Blake, it was like the honeymoon they never had.

As they lay in the feather bed in the middle of Paris, a view of the Eiffel tower out their window in the distance, Amy spooned close to Blake. She was always the first to make the move, but he never minded it.

"Paris, how romantic," she whispered.

"The city of love."

"And the city that I will love you in."

Amy melted into Blake's strong arms and closed her eyes as he kissed her. She knew this would be the way it would be for the rest of their lives. Loving each other, and Cooper too. Nothing could ever be better. To this day he could still feel her warm breath on his chest and her tender words, "I will love you forever."

*****

Cooper asked again, "Dad, what's for dinner?"

"Monsieur, as I said: Doigts de poulet avec frites français et."

Cooper, clearly irritated, crossed his arms. "Dad, please tell me in English, I'm starving."

"Very well, Monsieur. It's chicken fingers with French fries."

"Again?"

"Oui, again, Monsieur."

After dinner, the boys went to the park just down the street. There was just enough light from the surrounding buildings to see. Later, Cooper brushed his teeth, said his prayers, and bid Blake good night.

"Good night, Dad. I love you,"

"Thanks, Coop. I love you too."

On the way to his room, Cooper stopped by the front hall and kissed his mother's picture. "Good night, Mommy, in heaven. I love you."

Cooper retired to his room, formerly a closet, and turned the light off. There was no window and the door only closed partway because of the bed being in the way. Cooper suddenly remembered that he hadn't put his glove in its normal spot, atop a shelf in the closet, so he dashed out to retrieve it. That's when he heard it.

It was his dad. Ever so quietly weeping. Blake was holding Amy's picture close to his chest and softly speaking to her. "Babe, I'm so sorry that you are not here to see Cooper growing up. I'll never forgive myself for losing you. It was all my fault.

"You should see him. He's quite the guy. He made the team today. He was so thrilled, and so was I. To think, he's taking after his old man. And my old man before that. I only wish you could have been here to see his excitement. And I am so sorry that fate cut our lives short." Blake paused. "But don't worry, sweetheart, we are going to be fine. You are on my shoulder, and I am listening."

Cooper realized that this moment was a private one and that he should not disturb his grieving father, so he quietly went back to his bed for his own private cry.

The next day, like almost every day at school, McHenry was on Blake's back. This time he was ranting and raving about the library being in disarray. Several weeks before, Mrs. Clayton, the librarian, left on pregnancy leave and no replacement had been found.

McHenry approached: "Mr. Anderson. May I have a word?"

"Yes, Sir. Is there something you need?"

"Well, yes, now that you ask. I want you to come in on Sunday and see what you can do to straighten up the library. Since Mrs.

Clayton left, the place is an absolute pigsty. You know the type of families who send their children to this school. Do you think they're going to put up with a library that isn't first-rate? I don't think so."

"Sunday? Cooper and I have tickets for the Yankee game so we are tied up."

"Anderson, what time is the game?"

"Opening pitch is at 2:30. But Coop and I were going to have lunch at Mike's, that famous hot dog stand out in front of the park."

"Two-thirty, you say. So? Skip the dogs and come in around 8:30 A.M. You could leave for the game around one. That should give you lots of time to get to the stadium. Forget the dogs at Mike's and get a couple inside."

McHenry was at it again, trying to get his goat. Blake had to hold down his temper. He wouldn't lose it and give that ogre the satisfaction. He had his pride, and no two-bit jerk like McHenry was going to get to him. "Of course, why didn't I think of that, Mr. McHenry. Of course, I'll be there. Anything for St. Tim's." He decided he had to try to get McHenry's goat back. "That's, after all, why the board chose me to be vice principal."

CHAPTER SIX
FOUL BALL

THE DREADED EVENING FINALLY ARRIVED. KATHRINE DEL Monte was beside herself sorting every last detail. She had been to Bergdorf's four times before settling on the right dress. She opted for an off-the-shoulder Valentino black crepe dress that hugged her well-toned body. Kathrine had been at the gym for weeks getting down to a size four. The shoes by Christian Louboutin were shimmery silver, pricy at $3,400, and they matched the stunning diamond broach she wore on her shoulder. She spent the afternoon at Elizabeth Arden's Red Door getting "done" and two weeks ago arranged a stop at Dr. Abbott's for a lip plump. She wanted them perfect, just in case.

She had purchased the table, which allowed her to choose the guests. It was easy for her since she picked four other ladies, all widowed, older, and escorted by "walkers," a nice term for a gigolo. She let it be known that her date was not an escort but a "dear" friend from St. Tim's, vice principal no less. She lied and told her lady friends that she'd been seeing Blake and intimated that they were a lot more than hand-shaking friends.

The phone rang in Blake's apartment about two hours before the gala.

"Hello."

"Oh hello, darling, it's Kathrine, Kathrine Del Monte."

"Yes, Mrs. Del Monte. How are you?"

Kathrine bristled. "Listen, Blake, I insist that you call me Kathrine. Do you understand?" Then she softened her tone and added: "... darling?

Blake capitulated and agreed. "Of course, Kathrine, as you wish."

"Fabulous. Now I just wanted to give you a heads-up. You remember this is a black-tie event. You do have a tux, don't you?"

"Of course. When I was on Wall Street, my late wife and I attended many formal events." Sarcastically Blake continued. "It's an Armani if that's suitable."

"Armani! I just love Armani. Some of my favorite pieces are by him. You know I actually met him several times...but that's another story. Now let me tell you the plans...darling. My driver will pick you up at about seven. He will bring you to my place where I have invited a few friends for drinks before the gala."

Blake thought that wasn't part of the deal. The auction terms only called for his attendance at the Oktoberfest ball.

"Well, Mrs. ... I mean, Kathrine, the deal was the gala, not a cocktail party too." He tried to sound light. "I hadn't planned to be away from Cooper for that long."

"Oh stop, you're mine for the evening, and stop fretting, it's unbecoming.

Blake dropped the subject and decided to go along with this pushy woman's plan. After all, it was for charity and only one night. It wasn't like anything romantic was going to happen.

"OK. I'll be ready. I have a neighbor lady who will be babysitting Cooper, and she doesn't sit past midnight."

"Midnight, please, darling. What are you, a pumpkin? That is when all the fun begins. The crowd goes to Biff's for dancing and breakfast after the ball. You have to come!"

Blake knew of Biff's and that it was an ultra-exclusive millionaire's club hidden behind a secret door in the basement of The Sherry-Netherland hotel on Fifth Avenue. Lots of senior JP Morgan folks belonged.

"I'm afraid I can't. Mrs. Belinsky won't stay past twelve."

"Well, have the doorman look in on Cooper. I always do that when I'm out late and the housekeeper is off. He'll be just fine."

"Sorry, Kathrine, I don't have a doorman, and if I did, I wouldn't trust someone just checking on Cooper and not being here with him."

"Oh." Kathrine contemplated for a moment: "I've got it. Jesus will come over and stay with Cooper after that Mrs. What's Her Name leaves."

"Did I hear you right? You did say Jesus."

"Yes, Jesus."

"Um, are you for real? Jesus?" Blake thought, did she really think Jesus up in heaven was going to babysit.

"Oh, don't be silly. Jesus is my driver. He's from Puerto Rico and drives like a dream." Kathrine added, "He is handsome too, but a bit short for my taste. So, Cooper will be asleep and will never know a thing."

Blake couldn't believe his ears. This nut case wanted him to leave his only child until all hours in the morning with a total stranger, a driver he never even met. "Look, I'm truly sorry,

Kathrine, but that won't work. I don't care if Jesus, Mary, and Joseph show up, I'm not leaving Cooper with anyone I don't know."

"Oh Blakey, don't be a party pooper. Just go with the flow. I promise you a good time, and I do mean a good time."

"Sorry, Kathrine, my answer is no. I'll go to the ball, I'll even do drinks, but I'm home with Cooper at midnight."

Kathrine, realizing she wasn't going to have her way, something she was most definitely not used to, poutingly ended the conversation: "OK, Cinderella, home by twelve. Jesus will be there to pick you up, so be ready."

The phone clicked off.

The club was all that it was cracked up to be. Built by the Vanderbilts, the building was a replica of an Italian palazzo. The great hall towered five stories high and was topped by a magnificent stained-glass dome. It was the home away from homes for the super-rich. Drinks at Kathrine's were another eye-opener. Her townhouse was just a block or so away from the club on East 72nd Street. The intimate drawing-room was set up with a little bar manned by Arthur, the butler, who had a British accent and a black tux. He looked out of central casting.

The ride over had been another enlightening experience. Jesus showed up in a late-model Bentley right on time. A chilled bottle of Cristal champagne was sitting on a drop-down bar behind the driver's seat. He was a chatty sort.

"So, Jesus, you've been driving Mrs. Del Monte for a long time?"

"Oh, not that long. I was hired just before Mr. Del Monte passed away. He was ancient, but a good man to put up with her." Jesus realized he stepped over the line with that comment.

"Sorry, Sir. I didn't mean to say anything bad about Madam."

"Don't worry, nothing you and I say will be repeated."

"Thank you, Sir." Jesus looked at the rearview mirror and saw Blake's kind eyes. He was a handsome guy, the kind the madam most liked. "Do you know Madam for a long time?"

"Not really. I am the vice-principal at the school her children attend."

"Oh, St. Tim's. I go there every day when I bring the kids to school. Nice place."

"Yeah, it is. I love teaching there. My son attends too."

Jesus was puzzled that such a refined professional man like Blake would be one of those "hired bodies" that those old broads had.

"Will I be driving you home later or will you be spending the night, Sir? I didn't see an overnight bag."

"No way. Look, Jesus, I don't know why I feel I have to say this, but I'm here as a favor to the school. I have no intentions with your 'madam,' and she better not have any for me."

"I get it, Sir, And I am glad to hear you say it. You don't seem the type. Last month ... " He looked furtively around as if the limo might be bugged. "Well, the young man she invited home. ... He seemed very ... well, exhausted, Sir. After, I mean."

Blake worried if this night might come back and haunt him.

CHAPTER SEVEN
TELL ME ABOUT IT

ONE OF THE MOST SPECIAL TIMES BLAKE AND COOPER HAD was sharing meals together. No, it never was much to speak of; usually, something warmed up in the microwave or take-out from a cheap Chinese restaurant. Occasionally Blake would attempt pasta, doctoring up a store-bought sauce. Sunday, the boys splurged and usually made it to one of the local chains for a big brunch. But it wasn't about food. It was about the time they spent with each other. As Blake put it, "quality time." More than often the talk was about baseball, with Cooper eagerly paging through his well-worn Almanac. On other occasions, the two would dream out loud or just remember things that were important to them.

"OK, Dad, who holds the record for runs batted in?"

Blake sprung back with the answer. "… Hank Aaron 2,297."

"Right. Your turn." Blake didn't need the Almanac to come up with a good question. "All right, pal. How many baseball club managers are in the Cooperstown Hall of Fame?

Cooper hesitated. "That's a hard one. Let me think." He bit his lower lip, like he often did when thinking, just like Amy did.

" Oh, I know it. There were twenty-two club managers, as of last year inducted into the Hall of Fame. Oh, and ten umpires too.

"Brilliant, Coop."

In an attempt to keep the conversation going, Blake asked Cooper. " So, what's the latest thing you want to be when you grow up?"

Cooper didn't need a second to answer. "Dad, it never changes. First, I'd like to pitch for the Yankees, but that probably won't happen, so next I'd like to be just like you. A great dad and have a beautiful wife like Mom. And maybe two kids, 'cause having one is kinda lonely. That would be my dream."

Clearly touched emotionally, Blake smiled. "It's a great dream, and I have no doubt about it happening. Maybe not the pitcher part, but the other parts for sure."

"It's your turn. What do you dream for, Dad?"

Caught off guard when Cooper turned the tables on him, he seemed stumped for an answer. A long time ago, Blake's dreams ended. He knew that he had responsibilities, the most important of which was raising Cooper. But other than that, Blake feared to dream, because the dream that meant the most vanished in a towering inferno. "I don't know, Coop. I think I dream of you being my best buddy for the rest of my life…." Blake trailed off.

"Oh, Dad, that's not a dream. You already have that."

Blake cleared his choked-up throat and changed the topic. "So, Coop, it's your birthday in a couple of months. Do you have a special gift in mind?"

Cooper knew that what he really wanted was out of the question. He knew even at his tender age that his father had a hard time keeping them afloat, so he fudged the answer. "Oh, I don't know, maybe a glove or some new sneakers. Like the ones I saw in Walmart, they aren't expensive like the ones Deany Del Monte has. I really don't like them."

But Blake knew something that Cooper didn't. Cooper had confided in Mr. Como at the shop about what Cooper really wanted for his birthday. "Sneakers sound nice. But isn't there anything else you would rather have?"

Cooper fibbed. "No, just sneakers, and oh, maybe the glove."

"Well, Mr. Fibber. A little bird told me that what you really, *really* want for your birthday is a trip to Cooperstown Hall of Fame."

"Who told you that?" Cooper thought and then answered his own question. "I know, it was Mr. Como."

"Yeah, it was him."

"Look, Dad, I know that is out of the question this year, but maybe next. I can wait I'm only going to be nine, lots of time for that."

Blake was awestruck at Cooper's maturity and awareness. His little man was so perceptive. Probably inherited from his mother, not him. That, and having to grow up before his time when his mother vanished from their lives on that terrible day.

"I have an idea. If we are careful and I take Mr. Como up on some overtime he is offering, I think we can swing a short birthday weekend in Cooperstown."

"No, are you kidding, Dad? Really mean it?"

"Yes, I honestly do. But it depends on how much we can put aside until then. We have a couple of months, so I think we will be good."

"Oh boy, I can't wait." Cooper leaped up from the table and threw his arms around Blake. "You are the best, the very best, and I love you so much. Thank you, thank you!" Then he stepped back. "And the trip is cool and all, but I love you so much all the time, not just because you are taking me to the Hall of Fame."

Blake's cell phone rang, and he reached over to the counter to grab it. "Hello."

"Oh, hello. darling, it's Kathrine. How are you dear?"

Kathrine! Blake's stomach turned. The last thing he wanted was to talk to her. He cringed when he thought back to that disastrous evening at the Gotham Club and what followed.

Dinner was served after ten P.M. And the twenty-piece orchestra played classic swing tunes. The "walkers" were out on the dance floor like trained dogs waltzing around women, many of them decades older than they.

Kathrine made it a point to her lady friends that Blake was not an escort but a friend from St. Tim's who loved dancing and meeting new people. Blake looked great in his tux, which was exquisitely tailored and accented his physique, a point not unnoticed by the grand dames.

He recalled it was just after dinner and the orchestra started their second set.

"Come on, darling, they're playing our song."

Our song, what the blazes is she talking about. We don't have a song. I barely know this woman.

Kathrine grabbed Blake's hand and led him to the center of the dance floor. "Hold me tight, darling, I've had a few, and I don't want to fall."

Blake obliged thinking that should she fall, it would be even more embarrassing than having this middle-aged woman draped all over him.

Kathrine softly sang the words to Ray Charles's classic into Blake's ear: "I can't stop loving you …"

The slow dance seemed to drag on forever, and when Kathrine put her hand in Blake's pocket, he recoiled. "Look, Kathrine, I am so appreciative of your support for the school. But I think this is totally inappropriate. You are a parent and I am a teacher and an administrator at your children's school, and this kind of behavior is not only unprofessional but can create complications at school."

Kathrine totally ignored Blake's condonation and continued to finger the keys and loose change residing in his pocket.

Blake had enough. He abruptly stopped dancing, gripped Kathrine's arm, and briskly escorted her back to the table. "Excuse me, folks, but I just had a call from my babysitter, and there is a slight emergency at home."

One of the old ladies gasped. "Is everything all right? Is any-one hurt, dear?"

"Nothing serious, but I must excuse myself." Turning to Kathrine, Blake said: "Look, Kathrine, I'll find my way home and your driver can take you home, whenever …."

If looks could kill, Blake would be dead as a doornail. "If you must, darling." Turning to her friends, she whispered, "Kids, such nuisances; now I know why some species eat their young." Signaling a waiter, she ordered another martini and waved bye-bye as Blake left the ballroom. She turned to her lady friends and whispered. "He's delicious, isn't he?"

Blake couldn't wait to get out of that place. He walked briskly to the nearest subway station, knowing a cab to Brooklyn didn't fit into his budget. He caught the N train speeding toward Brooklyn and sanity.

When he arrived home, he thought that this would be the end of Kathrine Del Monte and her antics, but he later learned just how wrong he was.

On Monday, when Blake returned to St. Tim's, the school was abuzz. Apparently, the Del Monte kids had been spreading some made-up story about their mother and him. They had overheard her telling someone on the phone about the night at the Club. By the time lunch came, just about the entire school had heard how "hot" Mr. Anderson was and that he and Mrs. Del Monte were an item. This was just the kind of situation that played right into Mr. McHenry's hands.

McHenry spotted Blake in the teacher's lounge and with a sadistic grin walked up to him. "Anderson, you better stop in my office after lunch." The bitter and vindictive principal was having a heyday with these rumors.

Once in his office, McHenry began: "Anderson, what were you thinking? Mrs. Del Monte is a very important part of St. Tim's community. She is a parent with young children, and you are their teacher. Your behavior is appalling."

"My behavior! Exactly what are you talking about?"

"You know exactly what I'm talking about. Why those two poor Del Monte kids are telling everyone that their mother was practically seduced by you. They are traumatized."

"Nonsense. That never happened. The truth is that when Mrs. Del Monte bought that Gotham Club table at the fund-raiser she thought she bought me too and wanted her money's worth." Blake stopped and thought that what he just said sounded ridiculous, but it was true. "So, from the minute we met that night she threw herself at me like a two-dollar hooker on a slow night."

"Anderson, that's a terrible thing to say about someone like Mrs. Del Monte. She is lovely, a pillar to the St. Tim's community, not to mention the woman is a major donor to the school."

"Terrible thing to say? Well, I don't think you would be saying much nice about her, no matter how much money she gives, if she were in your pants pocket juggling your loose change and looking to grab the big enchilada."

"That's disgusting! Anderson, that was disgusting. You should know better and show more respect.

"Sorry, Sir, but that's the way it was. And as far as respect goes, I think Mrs. Del Monte could use some pointers."

"I'm afraid I'm obliged to take administrative action against you for these allegations."

"What?" Blake sat up in the chair. "Mr. McHenry, I told you this whole thing is fabricated by a very sick woman and repeated by a couple of super-entitled spoiled pre-adolescents who enjoy stirring the gossip pot."

"Nonetheless, this situation could turn serious. By some accounts, this borders on sexual harassment or worse. The school could have real liability. St. Tim's reputation could be at stake. So as a preventive measure, I'm going to place you on administrative probation for one year, effective immediately."

"You can't do that. I'm the victim here, not her."

McHenry smiled a victorious smile. He perhaps had found a path to getting rid of Blake. "Maybe you think you're the victim, but I'm the principal and make the decisions around here, and my decision is that you are officially on probation. Now, good day, Mr. Anderson. I have other matters to attend to ."

Blake left the principal's office and stepped into the anteroom where Angie sat with a look on her face that clearly meant she had heard every word of the conversation. And soon so would everyone else, starting with Nick the janitor and Alice the nurse.

Apparently, news traveled fast, so It wasn't long before Blake's phone rang. It was Kathrine.

Blake shook the memory from his head and listened carefully as she spoke. "You see, Darling, I heard some ghastly rumor that Mr. Henry placed you on probation. I can't believe it. Is it true?"

Blake had no use for this woman, so he intentionally was curt and to the point. "Yes, it's true, and you and your charming boys are responsible. It was some farfetched story your sons spread around the school that got me placed on probation. And you know, Mrs. Del Monte, the opposite of what they said is true."

"Oh, my poor darling." Kathrine paused to take a deep puff of her Benson & Hedges cigarette. "Those boys, they are always causing trouble. They get bored so easily and then stir things up just for the fun of it."

"Is there anything else, Mrs. Del Monte? I must go and attend to Cooper. To me, he's not a nuisance but a blessing."

"Yes, darling, there is. So don't go hanging up so fast. You see I can put a happy ending to this story and get your probation dropped."

Blake listened but did not respond.

"If you were, say, a little bit more interested in developing a, shall I say, friendship, things could be very different for you and, by extension, Cooper. I just need a little attention and some loving too."

Blake gagged with nausea. "Goodbye, Mrs. Del Monte."

"Not goodbye, Blake. No one says goodbye to me unless I want them to. We're not done yet." With that, she hung up.

Oh my God! Did this shrew really control his future?

CHAPTER EIGHT

FIELD OF DREAMS ... COME ON IN

FOR BLAKE, HAVING A PART-TIME JOB AT A BASEBALL MEMORAbilia shop was a dream come true. After Cooper, of course, baseball was his passion, and it was serendipitous how he came across this opportunity. Cooper and he had a pretty large collection of baseball cards. Nothing especially valuable, mostly current players, the collection was a fun activity they shared almost every day. One night on the way home from school, Blake had dozed off and missed his subway stop by two stations. When he realized it, he bolted from the train. Out of subway tokens he decided to walk the ten or so blocks home. At the top of the subway, exit stairs were a string of little shops. A mom-pop bakery, a knitting store, and a place called "Field of Dreams." The sign read: "Come on in." The shop owner was pulling down the shade that covered the tall dark-green wooden and glass doors just as Blake turned a brightly polished brass handle.

The shop owner addressed Blake. "Good evening, sir. I'm just about to close, but if you would like to take a quick peek around while I lock up, please do."

Mr. Como was a small older man with gray hair and oversized glasses. He seemed more like a bookkeeper or librarian than a baseball card enthusiast. Blake looked closer and saw his kind face and a broad smile as he spoke:

"So, you like baseball, yes?"

"Yeah, a lot. And so does my son."

The shop was filled with both new and vintage memorabilia. Glass cases held piles of clear plastic sleeves filled with trading cards. The walls had posters of all the famous players over the years. In one corner of the store was a tall cabinet, glass on three sides and locked. Blake peered through the doors and saw some pretty impressive collectibles. There was a signed glove of Joe DiMaggio's and an odd dozen or so balls all autographed by famous players.

"Those are my prize pieces. You like 'em?"

"Indeed. They must be very valuable."

"These? Not so much, but to me they are priceless. There are lots of things out there that are worth a fortune, but not mine. Let me introduce myself. I'm Renaldo Como, and I'm the proud owner here."

"How do you do, I'm Blake Anderson."

The two men shook hands, and Mr. Como said, "Nice to meet you, Blake. Feel free to take your time and look around. There is lots to see."

"Thank you, Mr. Como, but I see you were closing up, and I don't want to hold you from your dinner."

"Don't be concerned. Honestly, I have nowhere I must be. I'm a widower and live upstairs, alone."

Blake related immediately. "So am I, a widower that is, but I don't live alone. My young son and I live about ten blocks from here."

"Widowed? I'm so sorry. You are so young." Mr. Como was saddened and changed the subject. "Your son, does he like baseball too?"

"Like it? He lives and breathes it. I know he will be thrilled that I have stumbled upon your shop. I can't wait to bring him here."

"How old is your son?"

"Cooper is eight going on forty-eight. He is very mature in many ways. After his mother passed away, he's had to make a lot of adjustments."

"Sad, so sad. I know what loss is all about. I lost Lorretta, my wife, God bless her soul. We never had children but always wanted to. If we had they would be about your age now…maybe a few years older." Mr. Como looked Blake over and thought how proud he would be if someone like Blake were his son.

Blake glanced at his Rolex watch, a leftover from his high-flying days. "Oh, God, it's getting late. I must get back home. Cooper stayed home from school today, a bit under the weather, and Mrs. Belinsky is watching him. She'll be furious if I'm late, which I am already. I'd like to come back another time with Cooper."

"That would be wonderful. I'd love to meet another person who lives and breathes baseball." Mr. Como opened a case by the register and pulled out two packs of fresh baseball cards. "Here, bring these to your little boy. Tell him Mr. Como sent them and he looks forward to meeting him soon."

"Thank you, sir, but I insist on paying for them."

"Oh, no, young man, a gift is a gift, and paying for them is out of the question. Now, you better be on your way before that Mrs. Belinsky skins you alive."

Blake briskly walked the ten blocks home. He thought about Mr. Como and his sweet little shop. How lucky, he thought, to be doing something you love. That indeed was success by any measure. He also thought about how lonely Mr. Como looked. He knew that look because it was his perpetual expression too.

The apartment smelled wonderful as he opened the door. "I'm home, it's me!"

Cooper ran to greet his dad.

"How are you feeling, Coop?"

"I feel good, no fever and hungry. Mrs. Belinsky made us dinner. Doesn't it smell great?"

"Sure does." Blake took the few short steps to the kitchen just as Mrs. Belinsky pulled the homemade pierogis from the frying pan and smothered them with her delicious browned butter sauce. She knew they rarely had a home-cooked meal.

"I have to go home now and feed Mr. Belinsky, but I'll dish up your meal before I leave."

A generous heaping of pierogi and two thick slices of pot roast garnished with parsnips, carrots, and onions were put on mismatched plates. "Come on now, boys, sit down and eat before it gets cold. This is a dish we made in the old country." She sliced them both a piece of fresh bread she got at the bakery that morning. "Cooper, get the butter out of the frig," she instructed. "And the milk too."

Before leaving, Mrs. Belinsky tidied up the kitchen and gave her final instructions: "Now, Blake, all you have to do is the dishes;

everything else is cleaned and put away. And Cooper, you get a good night's sleep because you must go to school tomorrow. You are all better, I can tell."

Blake thanked Mrs. Belinsky and walked her to the door. "You are so kind, and I can't tell you how much what you do for us means." Blake opened his wallet and counted out the last of his bills; Ten, twenty, thirty-five. The graying old neighbor noticed that there wasn't any money left in his wallet. "Blake, will you do me a favor?"

"Of course, anything."

Mrs. Belinsky reached over and put the money back into Blake's hand. As she did, he noticed the tattooed number on her arm. A bleak reminder of her days as a Jewish Pole locked up in a concentration camp.

"Would you take this money back and get something nice for Cooper? He is such a great kid, and the last thing Mr. Belinsky and I need is money. We have enough for our needs. I should be paying you for taking care of Cooper. He's a joy."

"Oh, no, I couldn't. Please take the money."

"Don't argue with an old woman. Now, do as I say and put it away for Cooper."

"Well, since you put it that way, and you insist, I'll make an exception, just this once. Because if you don't take money for watching Cooper, I will feel bad asking you to."

"OK, it's a deal. But remember, I think I should be paying you. This is just too much fun."

On Sunday Blake and Cooper took the ten-block walk to Mr. Como's shop. The store opened at noon, so the boys had plenty of time for their Sunday morning pancake-fest. Cooper loved making the pancakes and had pretty much mastered the art of flipping them high in the air, with only an occasional miss as evidenced by a few stains on the ceiling. Layers of Nutella were slathered in between each pancake. When Blake could, he bought some fresh strawberries and whipped cream to top the stack. The pancakes were delicious, but even better was the fun they had in making them.

"Dad, what did you say the name of the shop was?"

"Field of Dreams."

"Like the movie?"

"Yeah, same name."

Cooper and Blake knew the movie well. They had watched it so many times that the disc was worn out.

"Does Kevin Costner own the shop?"

"No, Coop, he doesn't. A really nice grandpa-type man named Mr. Como does. I told him all about you. He was the one who sent you the baseball cards."

"Right. I remember you told me that."

They arrived at the store, and Cooper stopped to read the sign: "Field of Dreams…Come on in." "Cool, and look, Dad, the background on the sign is the same picture as on the movie cover…really cool.

"Good morning, gentlemen." Mr. Como greeted them as they walked into the shop.

"Good morning, Mr. Como. This is my son, Cooper."

"Hello, Sir, it's nice to meet you." Cooper extended his hand to shake. " And I want to thank you for sending me those baseball cards."

Blake swelled with pride. His little man had such good manners, and he didn't even have to be coached to show them off.

"My, aren't you a gentleman. Come in. Look around."

"Thank you."

Mr. Como walked next to Cooper. "Cooper, that's a great name. Is it a family name?

"Not really. My dad gave it to me. It's because he loves baseball and the Hall of Fame is in Cooperstown, so I guess he thought if I had that name, he'd always be close to it."

"I knew there must have been a connection. Have you ever been to Cooperstown?"

"No, neither has my dad. Someday, I really want to. How about you, Mr. Como. Have you ever been?"

"Oh yes, many times."

"Many times…. really? Wow.

"Well, Cooper, let me tell you a little secret. I didn't always own a baseball shop. In another life, I was a sportswriter. I went under the name Woody Whitmore. You see, according to my literary agent it was a better name than Como, which he thought was too Italian. Different days then; today it makes no difference what your name is.

Blake interrupted. "You're Woody Whitmore? I remember reading your columns. You were syndicated and printed even in Missouri, where I grew up."

"Royals, right? "

"Yeah, they were my team, but secretly I loved the Yankees."

After the many shop visits that followed, Mr. Como, Blake, and Cooper became fast friends. Cooper had gone to the library and found and read all of Woody Whitmore's columns. Mr. Como took great delight in spending hours telling Cooper about all the superstars he interviewed and wrote about.

Often customers would come in, some who knew who Mr. Como was in his past life. One such customer was a man named Rudy. He was even older than Mr. Como and loved to talk "ball."

Rudy was a regular and had his own stool at the counter where the customers would sit and chat with each other. Cooper mentioned to Mr. Como that his dad was looking for a part-time job to help with expenses and save up for a trip to Cooperstown. The old man thought he could probably use some extra help around the shop to get things sorted and to take care of customers when he had to be away or was resting.

So, when Blake was offered the job, he snapped it up. What a deal, he thought; extra money for doing something he loved. The customers love Blake, and the store had a whole new vibe, one of youth, laughter, happiness, and a bursting exuberance for the sport of baseball. The customers felt it, and business boomed. Over time Rudy became the shop's best customer and bonded with Blake. Soon, he increased his visits from occasional to regular and would follow Blake around the shop as he did his chores, and they would exchange stories and had a really great time. Rudy was fascinated that Blake played ball at Princeton with a full scholarship. He loved that Blake almost made the Major Leagues had it not been for an injury. Even after his Tommy John surgery, Blake's pitches didn't have the heat they once did. But he still loved to shag balls in the park. The best part for Rudy was Cooper, who often came along when his dad worked and whom he had come to adore as if he were his own. But there was so much more about Rudy that the dynamic duo was yet to learn.

CHAPTER NINE

"It Doesn't Matter Where You Sit as Long as You're There"

One of the perks of working at the baseball shop was the free tickets to Yankee games that came their way. Mr. Como, from past connections, was often given tickets to Sunday games and sometimes special playoffs. He loved to pass the complimentary tickets off to Blake and Cooper. Other times, Rudy dropped off tickets too. His were better seats and usually for regular games. He explained that a friend gave them to him and that he had problems climbing steps and being in large crowds so he didn't use them.

Often, Rudy would stop by the shop around four-thirty, and he and Blake would have coffee together at the next-door luncheonette.

Coffee at Aunt Bea's Luncheonette was never dull. Bea, a stout woman with a slight accent was in her late sixties and ran her luncheonette with the efficiency of a German engineering firm. Bea had emigrated from the fatherland some years after the war and settled in the Little Germany section of Brooklyn.

"Good afternoon, gents," Bea bellowed out as they entered the eatery. "I'll have your coffee in a second. Sit down. The afternoon paper's over there if you want."

"Thanks, Bea," the two chimed.

The coffee arrived, steaming hot in a cup and a half mug.

"Blake, pass the milk."

"Sure, Rudy." He slid over the silver creamer with its shiny handle. "Sugar?"

"No, thanks. My doctor is hounding me—says my sugar's a little high. But Blake, I don't know about you, but that apple strudel in that glass dome over there is calling out 'eat me.' Will you join me?"

"No Rudy. Thanks anyway, but if I had some of that, I'd have to spend another hour, which I don't have to spare, jogging around Brooklyn."

"Are you kidding me? You don't have an ounce of fat on you. I know a size-thirty-four waist when I see it."

"You're right on the money! How do you know?"

"Oh, I used to be in the rag business, years ago. After years of experience, you get to know what size people are. As for me, thirty-four is a long-gone number. The coffee is good, huh?"

"Very good." Blake thought back to his days of five-dollar cups of Starbucks. A habit he quit to save money. "I like it better than that Starbucks I used to drink."

"Starbucks?" Rudy reflected, "The guy who figured out how to extort five or six bucks for a cup of coffee is brilliant. I remember when coffee was a nickel, and the second cup was free."

Blake thought Rudy was an odd duck. Rudy knew a lot about a lot of things, especially about baseball. Every so often he would buy a couple of things at the shop, and other times he would bring in a piece or two for consignment sale. He seemed comfortable, money-wise, but never said too much about himself. He was a solitary, modest man with a warm and engaging smile, and that was good enough for him. Someday, maybe, Rudy would share his world, but for now, Blake would enjoy the coffee and baseball chats.

Bea strolled over. "So, Mr. Blake, how's Cooper?"

"He's great, thanks. And how are you doing, Bea?"

"Not bad for a fat old lady. My angina was acting up, but Doc Rosenberg said I'm good for another 100,000 cups of coffee." Bea laughed. "Hope he's right. So, boys, what's it going to be? I got fresh strudel, just made it this morning.... How about it?"

"None for me. Thanks, Bea."

"What about you, Rudy? It's still warm."

"Well, if you insist. Maybe a half-piece."

"Sorry, Rudy, I don't sell halves. It's all or none."

"OK, you talked me into it. Bring it on." Rudy grinned.

The heaping portion arrived on the thick, commercial plate, slightly discolored from thousands of times in the dishwasher.

"There you go. Enjoy." Bea topped off their coffees.

And Rudy did enjoy it: immensely, every bite of it. When he was done scraping his plate to collect up the last morsel of filling, Blake poked him in the arm. "Looks like that half of piece wouldn't have done. Ha-ha."

Rudy's eyes twinkled and then he dug into his jacket pocket and pulled out two tickets. "Here, Blake, I won't be using these, and I thought you and Cooper would like to see the game. It's the Yankee-Red Sox game."

"Wow, Cooper will be so excited. Thank you, Rudy, thank you! Our nemesis! The Red Sox!"

Blake looked over the tickets and realized they were special seats. "Legends Suite? God, Rudy these are the best seats in the house, behind home plate, Section 14A. Where the hell did you get these? They're like gold."

Rudy smiled and gave Blake a wink.. "Oh, I have friends, and they are always good to poor old Rudy. But how do you know about these seats?"

"Oh, Cooper and I play baseball trivia constantly. We use the Almanac to look up questions and answers. Information is not just about ballplayers, but about ballparks too. Like the best seats or how far it is to the dugout from one place to another, stuff like that is all in there. That's how."

Blake listened while Rudy gave him a peek into his background. "You see, Blake, my father, got in the rag business when he came to America. For years he worked altering expensive clothes in Bergdorf Goodman's, a fancy department store for the super-wealthy. The founder, Herman Bergdorf, and my father both came from the same place in Germany, a place called Gadenstredt, and Mr. Bergdorf hired him because of that. The store was a huge success and Bergdorf became extremely wealthy. In a gesture of kindness, from one kinsman to another, he gave my father a stake, like a loan, to get into his own business. For years my father struggled, and eventually, I joined the firm right out of high school. Business got a lot better and well... the rest is, well, the rest...." Rudy paused. "Mr. Bergdorf was a really kind man and never forgot his roots. You know he's buried right here in Brooklyn, in Cypress Hills Cemetery, just a short walk from here. Funny, it's the same place my father is buried too. They were close friends here on earth and now are just a few feet away, in death."

Blake was glad to learn a little more about Rudy. But his story really didn't explain his passion for baseball and how he had access to such special tickets to games.

Cooper couldn't wait to get to the game.

Cooper asked Mr. Como: "Why do the Red Sox fans hate the Yankees so much."

"Well, it goes back to January 5th, 1920, when Harry Frazee, the Sox owner, sold Babe Ruth to the Yankees. Babe was a star, but Frazee didn't like the Babe and made the sale anyway. After the sale, the Red Sox did not win a World Series for eighty-six years. This led to the superstition known as the 'Curse of the Bambino,' which was one of the main reasons the rivalry exists."

The VIP seats came with a bunch of perks. Free drinks, Coke for Cooper, all the hot dogs they could eat, and a massive foam rubber finger with the Yankees logo.

Cooper loved it all.

"Rudy is really nice isn't he Coop?"

"Yeah, he is, You don't think he's weird or maybe a zombie in disguise, do you?"

"A zombie! Really, Cooper, what a screwy thing to say. No, Rudy is a kind and gentle old man who likes baseball like you and me."

Cooper thought some more; yea, that was pretty stupid to say. I've been watching too much TV. I guess he's more like a grandpa than a zombie."

Cooper didn't know much about his grandparents. Both sets of grandparents were either far away unable to be part of their lives, or deceased. Amy's mom, devastated by her daughter's death, spoiled Cooper from afar and sent birthday cards, postcards, and Christmas cards. They talked on the phone. But it wasn't like getting to hang out with Mr. Como and Rudy, Mr. and Mrs. Belinsky, and even Bea.

"Gee, Dad, these are great seats. How did Rudy get them?"

"He really didn't say. He's sort of quiet about stuff."

"I wonder why he just gives the tickets away. He could sell them for a lot of money, probably."

"Yeah, he could. But maybe to him having you enjoy them is worth far more than any money he could get by selling them."

"Really? But he doesn't even get to see me enjoying them."

"He doesn't need to. For some, just knowing things is enough."

The seats were even better than the ones Blake got from JP Morgan and way better than the ones Mr. Como often gave them. But, as Cooper always said, "Dad, it don't matter where you sit as long as you're there."

Blake, of course, corrected him: "You mean, 'It *doesn't* matter where you sit.'"

Cooper replied, "Yeah, Dad, that's what I said, it 'don't matter.'"

Blake dropped the effort to grammatically correct Cooper and focused on the larger meaning of what Cooper's youthful wisdom really meant.

It doesn't matter where you sit … as long as you are there. How poignant. Wasn't that the truth? Wasn't that what life was all about? Showing up and being there.

Had Rudy figured that out? Mr. Como too. Perhaps. Would he?

CHAPTER TEN
THE TOILET CZAR

MONDAY MORNING TURNED INTO ANOTHER FIASCO BACK AT St. Tim's. Sam showed Blake a printer-ready proof of the upcoming yearbook. It had been reviewed by the various faculty members and approved by Mr. McHenry. The final proof included caricatures of multiple teachers and staff members with funny captions. Nurse Alice was depicted as a mad surgeon; Angie, the secretary, as a sexy stenographer with legs up to her armpits; Mr. McHenry holding the keys to a door marked "opportunity"; and Blake holding his nose sitting on a commode, wearing a crown with the title "Toilet Czar." The title had been added by Mr. McHenry in his own handwriting. His approving initials clearly authorized the edit.

Blake burst into Mr. McHenry's office, holding the proof. "Excuse me, Sir, but could you please explain this?" He threw the proofs on the principal's desk.

McHenry picked up the proof, looked over, and spoke. "Explain what?"

"The pictures, cartoons, whatever they are."

"Oh, those." He laughed. "The student editors are just poking fun at us. Don't be so thin-skinned."

"I don't think it's just the staff poking fun, Mr. McHenry. Clearly, the title added on the crown is in your handwriting and your initials indicate an approved edit."

"Like I said, Mr. Anderson, don't be such a drama queen. It's funny. Everyone will laugh and pat you on the back for being such a good sport."

"Well, it's not funny to me; it's demeaning. If you don't get this changed, I'm going to the board and tell them of your constant vindictiveness and harassment and that you are trying to embarrass me."

"Sit down, Anderson. Sit over there," McHenry pointed to the empty chair in front of his desk. "Now, Anderson. *You* need to understand that I call the shots at this school, no one else. And that if I decide to have a picture of you or anyone else in the yearbook, it will be printed. Further, if you think I'm worried that your bellyaching to them will intimidate me, you are just flat wrong. So, remember who the boss is here and don't threaten me. I don't scare easily. Lastly, might I remind you, you're on probation so one wrong move and your O.U.T. Do you understand, Anderson? Now get out of my office and get back to work."

Blake stood up, grabbed the proof, and stormed out. He could almost swear he heard McHenry say: "Woosh."

Angie's ears were ringing as she reached for the phone.

That night, Blake made a rare call to Stu. "Hi Stu, it's Blake Anderson."

"You don't have to tell me who it is. I'd know that voice anywhere. What's up, brother?"

"I've got a tricky situation on my hands, and I hate to circumvent the system, but this guy McHenry is trying to humiliate me in front of the whole school, students, faculty, and parents alike."

Blake went on to explain the situation and how McHenry, time and time again, overstepped his authority and was hell-bent on making Blake's life miserable with the unspoken intention of getting him to resign or be terminated.

"Wow, Blake, That's nasty. McHenry is a known entity at St. Tim's and has done a good job for a long time. But this, well, this is indefensible. Exactly what do you want me to do?"

"Look, Stu, I love it at St. Tim's. Cooper does, too. And the free tuition is critical. I think I do a pretty good job too."

Stu interrupted: "No, you do an excellent job. And everyone loves you." Stu corrected himself, "Well, everyone but you know who."

"Yeah. And I really don't know why he has such contempt for me. I do my best to accommodate his every directive, even the most ridiculous and demeaning ones. I do my job with professionalism, and I am completely dedicated to the school's mission: 'Educating and nurturing students.'"

"Like I said, Blake, what do you want me to do? I'm happy to try and help."

Blake didn't want to put Stu in a compromising position by asking him to have the board discipline or possibly terminate McHenry. It would be one of those "him or me" situations, and they never work out well. Blake took a deep, measured breath and decided to avoid a showdown.

"Stu, if you can get McHenry to back off on printing that yearbook picture and perhaps have someone on the board can pull him aside and tell him to lay off with his inordinate disdain for me, it might help."

Stu, without hesitation, agreed. "Done. I'll see to it. It will be either the chairwoman or me."

On Friday afternoon, Mr. McHenry made it a point to corner Blake on the sports field. "Anderson, you're dead meat. Whining to the board must have been a death wish. You are already on probation, which makes you one step away from the exit door. So, you better buy a calendar and start checking off the days you have left at St. Tim's." McHenry turned and strutted off, leaving Blake alone on the field.

Well, Blake thought. *That sure worked out .... who knows what's next?*

CHAPTER ELEVEN
Happy Birthday Da ...

The school year was nearing an end and St. Tim's was aflutter with activities. McHenry assigned Blake the task of running the graduation exercises knowing that it was a job filled with anxious parents, tired faculty, and kids that were generally off the wall with excitement. He called Blake to his office to give him the news. Blake walked into the office anteroom and was greeted by Angie's broad smile.

"Good afternoon, Mr. Anderson."

"Hello Angie, how are you today?

"I'm fine, thank you. I must say you look quite handsome today, and I love your hanky."

Blake was wearing a well-tailored blue blazer that he got as a birthday present from Amy. The birthday just before she died. This was the first he could bring himself to wear it. But he forced himself in the name of moving on. The blazer had a story just like everything else he and Amy shared, and it instantly flashed through his mind.

*****

"Happy birthday, sweetheart." Amy threw her arms around Blake as he walked through the door and kissed him.

"Sorry, I'm late, babe, but a last-minute meeting came up."

A thunderous stampede of footsteps came running from a bedroom down the hall.

"Happy Birthday, Daddy," shouted an excited Cooper joining the couple in a group hug.

"Come on in, Daddy, and see what I made you for your birthday."

Cooper had been a busy boy. When he came home from school he and Amy had baked and decorated a cake to surprise him. Amy wasn't really a baker, and Cooper had never tried before, so the results were more of an excellent effort than a culinary triumph.

Blake walked over to the dining room table and beheld their masterpiece. "Wow, look at that. It's, it's … it's unbelievable. You made this?"

"Yeah, but Mommy helped. I mixed everything up and poured it into the pans. Then I remembered I forgot the eggs, so we had to dump it out of the pans and back into the bowl. When we were finished, Mommy put it into the oven because she was afraid I would burn myself."

Blake turned to Amy and nodded. "Very smart, that Mommy of yours."

"Of course, she is! Then when it was done, we had to wait a really long time before we could decorate it. When it was cool, we took it out of the pans and put it on this nice dish."

"Honey," Amy interrupted. "It's a cake stand. That's what you call it."

"Yeah, a cake stand, not a dish." Cooper wondered, "What the heck is the difference anyway?"

Blake walked over and took a closer look at the cake, iced in white frosting with blue lettering, and read the inscription out loud: "Happy Birthday Da."

"Oh, sorry, Dad, we ran out of blue frosting, so I couldn't finish "DADDY."

Blake held back his laughter so as not to diminish Cooper's efforts and looked at Amy. "It's great. Thank you so much, both of you."

Blake recalled that the cake tasted much better than it looked, and how Cooper kept putting his fingers in the icing and sneaking a taste.

"Let's give Dad his presents," urged Cooper. "Open mine first."

Blake took the small box from Cooper and put on a show, taking his time to untie the ribbon and remove the gift wrap.

"Come on, Daddy, open it." A beside-himself Cooper coached.

Inside the box was a handsome faux silk pocket square. It was navy blue with small white baseballs printed throughout. "Oh, I love it, Cooper, I really love it. Where did you ever find anything like this?"

"Mom and I went shopping last week and found it in that little store just off Time Square, you know the one, the one with all the Yankee stuff in the window. The one we bought some cards from."

"Of course, I know that store. It's one of my favorites."

Cooper shone with pride and was delighted that his father loved the gift he had so carefully picked out. "And I paid for it with my own money!"

"I'm touched, little man, really touched. Thank you," Blake picked up Cooper and hugged him dearly.

Amy handed Blake another box. This one much larger and heavier. "This is from me. Nothing as exciting as Cooper's gift, but something I think you will like."

"Saks Fifth Avenue," Blake read off the box. "Fancy-dancy!"

Blake opened the box and removed a fabulous blue cashmere blazer with monogrammed brass buttons. "Oh, I love it," he exclaimed. "It's really beautiful."

*****

Blake was brought back to the moment when he heard Angie say. "The boss will see you now."

"Sit down, Anderson. I have an assignment for you."

Blake took a deep breath and awaited yet another task to add to his staggering load. He already had the baseball team in the finals with Mount Christian School, which required away games and his math exams to give and correct plus all the extra-help sessions he was committed to doing.

"I'm putting you in charge of graduation this year. Miss Pennyworth is worn out, she's been doing it for years, and quite frankly, she's done. So, I'm handing the job over to you."

Blake offered him an impassive stare to show him he was getting used to him being an utterly hateful jerk. "Sure, *boss*." His voice dripped with condescension.

"This year is St. Tim's Diamond Anniversary, our seventy-fifth year. Graduation is important, and parents' expectations are sky-high. After all, they have to spend a small fortune educating their kids and expect a crescendo moment in time as their little darlings leave the hallowed halls of St. Tim's. But this year being our seventy-fifth, the bar is set even higher.

Blake could hardly bear the drama coming out of this man's mouth.

"You can speak with Miss Pennyworth, but I expect something far more exciting than the dull old dog and pony show she's been dishing up for years. I want the parents and the kids to have an exceptional experience. And it's up to you to come up with it." McHenry paused. "Unless you're not up to the task. If you aren't, I'll have to advise the board that you can't do it, and I'll have to pick someone else who can meet the challenge."

Blake realized what McHenry was up to. He was handing him a very difficult job…one that had potential failure written all over it, and almost a certain set-up. If he declined, he would be made to look uncooperative or, worse, incompetent. McHenry put him into an untenable situation. Blake knew that there were so many things on his plate, especially at the end of the term, and adding this one was going to make his life even more stressful.

"Oh, yes, Anderson, as part of the festivities, there will be the night-before potluck dinner in the gym when the student awards will be made. You'll have to manage that too. And, by the way, you better make sure that the 'right' kids get awards.

"So, Anderson, what will it be? Are you going to step up to the plate, pardon the pun, or are you the loser I always thought you were and make me tell the board."

Blake took the high road. Rather than look defeated, duped, and abused, he would accept the challenge with robust eagerness. "Mr. McHenry, thank you *so much* for this opportunity. I just *love* working for you. And I've always loved graduations, and some great ideas popped into my head as you were speaking. I know I can do this and make this year's graduation at St Tim's the best ever! Thank you."

McHenry sat and just stared at Blake. Had he just been checked? "Get out of my office; we're done here."

Blake rose to leave and left, and McHenry pledged: "Anderson, your ass is grass if you flub this up."

Blake turned, pulling himself to his full height. He smirked and looked at McHenry with all the condescension he could muster. "You watch," he audibly muttered under his breath as he walked out.

"What did you say?" McHenry snapped.

"Oh, I wasn't speaking to you." And with that, Blake opened the door and departed with a friendly smile to Angie. "See you at Graduation…."

CHAPTER TWELVE
For Now and Through Eternity

The potluck dinner got rave reviews. Mrs. Belinsky was drafted to make a variety of her old-world dishes, which were scoffed up by the chic parents in record speed. Aunt Bea provided a truckload of home-baked European desserts, and Rudy donated the money for a three-piece combo. When the awards were presented, contrary to Mr. McHenry's edict, they were given to the deserving students, regardless of how much money their families had given to the school. There were two highlights to the awards ceremonies. The first was the St. Tim's baseball team had come in first in their division with three consecutive no-hitters. Each of the team members proudly walked to the stage for their trophies.

The second was that the school's highly sought-after teacher-of-the-year award was unanimously awarded to Blake. Mr. McHenry was beside himself with rage and jealousy.

Graduation followed the next day, and Blake staged the grandest one imaginable. With the help of Kathrine Del Monte, yes, her. He knew that it was a risk since she probably would be calling in the favor, but he chanced it. Kathrine twisted a lot of arms and managed to work miracles. She coerced the director of Lincoln Center to volunteer their concert orchestra to play "Pomp and Circumstance," along with a musical tribute to St. Timothy, the school's patron saint. Further, Kathrine, knowing that the Gotham Club was having a gala the night before graduation was able to get them to donate the fabulous floral arrangements to the school. The cost alone for those flowers she knew exceeded $12,000. Stu, a devoted parishioner and supporter of St. Thomas Episcopal Church on Fifth Avenue, "convinced" the Archbishop to give both the invocation and benediction.

But the coup de grâce was when Ralph Du Pont, Deputy Mayor of New York City, a fellow Princetonian and Sig brother gave the commencement address.

Blake smirked seeing McHenry's face. It was worth the effort to watch the pathetic principal seethe in his seat while having to plaster a smile on his face for the parents.

Friday, the last day of school, couldn't come too soon. Blake was exhausted and had just about enough of St. Tim's and Mr. McHenry. On Saturday, Mrs. Belinsky offered to take Cooper for an overnighter to play with her grandson, Morris. The kids had played before and got on well. Blake took the opportunity to sleep in late and relax. Later in the afternoon, he decided to take on a task he had put off far too long because it was a heart-wrenching job. Tucked away on a high shelf in Cooper's closet/bedroom were three boxes of Amy's effects. When he and Cooper moved out of their midtown apartment, Blake asked their cleaning lady to box up Amy's things, excluding her clothing, which he told

Carla to take for herself as they were about the same size. Each box was labeled: Miss Amy's.

Blake opened the first box, which contained some of Amy's favorite books, a sterling silver Parker pen, and many letters that apparently Amy saved. The letters were mostly from her best girlfriend in London and some fewer from various friends. Blake found a half dozen congratulatory cards that they received when Cooper was born. He continued to rummage around and thought: *this isn't as bad as I thought it might be,* until he came across a program from their wedding. Tucked in the program was a legal-size piece of paper, folded in half. Blake opened it carefully and saw a handwritten draft that apparently Amy prepared. On the top page was the title: Vows. Blake began to read:

> *I, take you, Blake Thomas Anderson, to be my husband, my best friend, my lifetime partner, and the one and only love of my life.*
>
> *I vow to comfort and inspire you from this day forward for the rest of my life.*
>
> *I will forever be there to laugh with you and to hold your hand in times of sunshine and in moments of darkness. I shall mother your children and grow old with you always with unconditional love.*
>
> *You are my one and only, my inspiration, and my hero. On this day our hearts will become one and our souls inseparable.*
>
> *You are my Love, my being, my everything, for now and through eternity.*

Deep in his memory, Blake could hear Amy saying these vows. Reading them again now, it was more than he could bear.

On Sunday, he showed up early for his shift at Field of Dreams.

Mr. Como took one look at Blake and asked: "What happened to you? You look like you lost ten pounds and have circles under your eyes."

"Oh, I'm fine, really. It was just hectic the last few days of school, and well, I'm just exhausted." What Blake didn't tell Mr. Como was that he had only a few hours of sleep after going through Amy's things.

"You look too tired to work here today. Go home!" insisted Mr. Como. "Don't worry, I'll pay you for the day. I know you need the money for that birthday trip to Cooperstown. That's the weekend of the Legends Game. It's gonna be great, Cooper will love it!"

"I'm just fine. Now let me get to work." Blake paused: "You know, Mr. Como, I really don't consider what I do here work. It's more like spending time with friends and family, and being among all this baseball stuff… that's not work, it is precious time for me."

Cooper arrived home on Sunday and couldn't wait to plan the trip.

"Dad, have we saved up enough money to go to Cooperstown for my birthday? It's only a few weeks away."

"I think so, but we will have to be careful about how we spend."

"No problem, I'll pack lunch, and we won't have to stop on the way. And I won't ask for a thing, I promise."

Blake hated that Cooper had to worry about anything, especially money.

"I do have some good news, Coop."

"What?"

"Sam at school said we can borrow his car for the trip."

"Wow, that will save a lot of money, right?"

"Yeah. And Coop, I bet you can't guess what kind of car he has. I think you'll love it."

"A red Mercedes convertible?"

"I see you have fancy taste." Blake laughed. "Well, you are partially right."

"It's not a convertible?"

"No, actually it is. But it's not a Mercedes."

"Oh." A glint of disappointment crept into his voice but instantly disappeared. He was grateful for any kind of car.

"It's, ready for this, a Mini Cooper!"

"No way."

"Yes, way… and we have it for the whole weekend. And oh yeah, it actually is red."

Cooper pulled out the brochures that the tourist office had sent. "There is so much to do there, Dad. I can't wait." He held up one of the brochures. "Look at this place…. It's a palace or something."

Blake took a look. "That's the Otsego Resort Hotel, but we definitely can't stay there. Let's keep looking."

Blake rifled through the brochures and found one for the Cooper's Inn. Even better, there was a coupon for fifty percent off. "Hey, Coop, how about this place?"

"Looks, cool. Like a fancy old house. The bricks are really red, and I like the front door."

Blake marveled at Cooper's attention to detail. "Shall I give them a call?"

"Now?"

"Yeah, now! Why not?"

The day before the boys left for Cooperstown, Blake did a shift at the shop. Mr. Como was almost as excited as Cooper about going. He had compiled a stack of guidebooks for them to take. Around four o'clock Rudy showed up for a coffee.

"Hi Rudy, good to see you."

"Thanks, Blake. So, are you all set to go?"

"I doubt Cooper will sleep tonight."

"I'll bet. And you?"

"I must admit, I'm excited too. I always wanted to go to the Hall of Fame when I was a kid in Missouri, but it was so far away and expensive to get to. When I came East, I played ball at Princeton, but never had the chance to go. Once I started working and could afford a trip … well there never was time. Between Amy's job and mine and school for Coop, we just never got around to it."

"Cooper will never forget this birthday. And you, Blake, are the one making it memorable. Speaking of birthdays, here's a little something for Cooper." Rudy handed Blake an envelope with a debit card enclosed.

"Oh, Rudy, you don't have to do that, really."

"Of course, I don't, but I want to. And Cooper is special. It's just a small token gift that will come in handy. Now let's go get some coffee at Bea's.

Bea had been waiting for Blake to come by that afternoon.

"Well, look what the cat dragged in. Sit down, I'll be right with you."

The two had their coffee, and Rudy splurged on a couple of pieces of homemade rugelach.

Bea came over to the counter with a large white box. "These are some chocolate chip cookies I made for your road trip. And two birthday cupcakes to celebrate Cooper's big day."

Bright and early that Friday morning the Mini Cooper was packed and ready to go. Cooper wanted to sit in the front seat, but Blake would have no part of it. "Sorry, Coop. You aren't a hundred pounds yet. Can't be in a seat with airbags. It's too dangerous for you upfront, and besides, I think it's against the law."

Reluctantly Cooper agreed and made himself comfortable in the small back seat. His backpack, Game Boy, the Baseball Almanac, and the large bakery box from Aunt Bea's filled the empty seat next to him.

The ride was a long one, some three and one-half hours. The boys laughed raucously at the irony of Cooper, going to Cooperstown in a Mini Cooper. To fill up the time Cooper and his dad played endless baseball trivia. When Cooper had had enough of that, they played license-plate bingo followed by a sing-along with every song that Cooper knew, with "Take Me Out To The Ball Game" multiple times. Just before Albany, Blake pulled into a service center to fill up. He fished around for some cash and came across the debit card from Rudy and remembered his words. "Use this to help on the trip." The cashier processed the card and gave him the receipt showing the balance of $473.13. Blake silently thanked his dear friend for his generosity. This amount of money would help make the trip not as much of a financial strain. He could relax a little knowing if Cooper wanted a souvenir or a nice meal, he could. For the millionth time, it seemed, he was so grateful for the good people surrounding him and Cooper.

With less than an hour to go, Cooper dozed off, and Blake finally had some quiet time.

He thought about Amy and how she would have enjoyed this trip. No, he knew she wasn't cockeyed crazy for baseball like Cooper and him, but she would have cherished seeing Cooper light up when he finally got to see the Hall of Fame. Blake could only imagine Cooper's pain of being motherless, especially on his birthday; it saddened him. But he didn't have to imagine his own pain, the one in his heart, as he drove through life without his co-pilot in the passenger seat. As bad as he felt, he resolved not to let it ruin their time and Cooper's birthday.

As they arrived in Cooperstown, they drove down Pioneer Street towards Main. Cooper had woken about fifteen minutes earlier and was beyond excited. They drove by beautiful Victorian homes with emerald lawns and perfusions of colorful flowers.

"Where is it, Dad?"

Blake knew what it was that Cooper meant. "It's at the end of Main Street, according to this map. We should be seeing it pretty soon."

The bright red Cooper turned onto Main Street, which was a picture of Americana. Huge baskets of cascading flowers hung from dozens of wrought-iron lamp posts on both sides of the street. Colorful American flags mounted on many of the shops waved gracefully in the breeze. About halfway down the street, a massive flagpole rose in the center of a rotary, and just a few yards down, on the right, Cooper, saw for the first time the Hall of Fame.

Blake looked back through the rearview mirror and caught sight of something that would be indelibly etched in his memory.

Cooper had opened his backpack and pulled out his mother's picture and held it against the window. "Look, Mom, we made it. Look, it's the Hall of Fame."

CHAPTER THIRTEEN
I'M REALLY HERE!

THE MINI COOPER STOPPED IN FRONT OF THE HALL OF FAME, and Cooper rushed out. "Dad, I'm really here, and so are you. Can we go in?"

"Yes, but let's start fresh tomorrow. It's after lunchtime, and we should eat. But first, we need to check into the Inn."

"Gee, I was hoping we could go in now."

"Coop, I promise, you will have the entire day tomorrow to see it, and everything else. We have three days, lots of time."

Cooper reluctantly agreed and piled back into the Mini.

The car slowly approached the historical Cooper Inn. A stately iron fence surrounded the property, and lush green lawns bordered the parking area.

"Look, Dad, just like the picture in the brochure, even better. It's beautiful!"

"Sure is."

Blake parked the car under a tall oak tree. The lot was almost full, and the parking slots were tight. Blake grabbed the suitcase, and Cooper collected his backpack and assorted things he had brought. They walked the short distance to the elegant stairs that led to the entrance flanked by flowerpots. Much of the front of the inn was covered with dark green ivy carefully cut to allow for window and door openings. Under most of the front windows were window boxes each bursting with bright fuchsia, pink, purple, and white perennials. English Ivy cascaded down from each of them ending in graceful curls.

Cooper ran up the steps and waited for his father who lagged behind enjoying the antiquity of this historical place. "Come on, Dad. I want to see inside. And I'm hungry."

Cooper opened the large door finished in high-gloss black paint, surrounded by bright white shutters, and walked in. "Holy smokes, look at this place."

A sudden flash of concern gripped Blake as he thought that the Inn looked way more expensive than he could afford. But he remembered he had a hotel confirmation in his pocket with a firm guaranteed discounted room rate.

A young man behind a small reception desk greeted him: "Good afternoon, Sir, my name is William. May I assist you?

Blake pulled out the folded-up confirmation and presented it to the desk clerk. "We have reservations, the name is Anderson, Blake Anderson, and Cooper."

"Yes, Sir, we have been expecting you."

The clerk sorted the check-in, and Blake was instructed that the room was on the third floor in the back. There was no elevator so the boys hiked up the grand circular staircase to the second floor. Once there, they walked to the back of the hall, as directed, they found a secondary staircase leading to what the confirmation referred to as "attic accommodations."

At the top of the stairs was another hall with four doors, three marked with numbers and one marked "Lavatory."

"We're in room three, Cooper."

The boys entered the room and looked around. Two twin beds, an almost miniature dresser, and a comfortable reading chair. The room was small, immaculate, and had everything they needed.

Blake knew when he booked that "bargain" rates did not mean getting a posh room normally found in a first-class establishment like this. Every hotel has price points, and room three was entry-level.

"Well, buddy, it's not the Ritz, for sure, but we came for the baseball, not for sleeping, and besides, when the lights are out all rooms are the same."

"I suppose you're right." Cooper looked around and asked, "Where's the bathroom?"

"You didn't see it?"

Cooper looked around some more. "I don't see it. It's not even here."

"Right, again. It's in the hall. Didn't you see the door marked 'Lavatory'?"

"Yeah, I saw it, but I thought it was to a science lab or something."

"It's the bathroom, and it's just across the hall, and when you need it, you know where it is. Now, come on, let's find a place to eat."

"Cool, and could we get some ice cream and ride around too?"

"Sure."

Cooper tore down the back staircase and headed towards the elegant circular one leading to the lobby.

"Slow down, Tiger. It's not polite to run, especially in a fancy place like this. Walk like a gentleman."

Cooper took Blake literally and pranced down the stunning staircase like a king might, stopping at each step and looking around. "Cut it out, Cooper, you're such a ham."

The boys stepped out of the Inn and noticed a bit of a commotion in the parking lot. It was just inches away from their borrowed bright red Mini.

Blake looked closer and put his hand to his head. "I don't believe it. Some moron backed into the car."

Cooper was frightened because he knew the car wasn't theirs, and his dad would be responsible if anything happened to it. He worried this could ruin their trip.

An attractive woman was talking to the young desk clerk who check them in.

"I'm so sorry, Billy. I have no idea whose car this is, but you must find out for me. I want to be certain that I take care of the damage."

"I'll check, Miss Mason. When people check in, I get their vehicle information for the record. So, if the owner is a guest, I'll find him."

Blake walked up to the twosome.

"Excuse me, I'm Blake Anderson, and this is my car. Well, actually, it's not. What I mean to say it's my friend's car, and he loaned it to me."

"Oh, Sir, I'm so sorry, but I didn't see your car and I backed my truck into it." Lois paused to take a breath. "And don't worry, I have insurance, and they will take care of all damage."

Blake looked over the car. "Well, it looks like the damage is superficial. That's good."

"Thank God. I'm so sorry; it was all my fault. I was in a hurry and was being careless."

"Oh, I know you didn't mean it. But you see it's my friend's car, and he lives in the city. Getting anything fixed there is a nightmare. I think he'll be quite upset with me when I return the car damaged."

"Upset? With you? Certainly not. It was me who was careless."

Blake looked away from the Mini and took a second look at this woman. She was about his age, maybe a couple of years older. She was attractive with high cheekbones and pretty brown hair that bounced off her shoulders. She reminded him of the girls he knew in high school back in Missouri—that all-American look. Very pretty, but not beautiful. Wholesome was the word that came to mind.

Cooper came running over and touched the damaged back fender. "Boy, is Sam going to be mad."

Blake grabbed Cooper's hand and attempted to assure him Sam would not be angry—they'd just have to get it fixed.

"After all, Coop, it was an accident, no one got hurt, and it's not the end of the world. We'll figure this out, don't worry."

The woman took notice of how well this good-looking father was handling the boy's worry. She also noticed how cute Cooper was and how the two, father and son, seemed to have noticeable chemistry.... A loving connection.

She said: "Look, Mr. ..."

"It's Anderson, Blake Anderson, and this is my son Cooper."

Cooper stuck out his hand and shook. "Nice to meet you, Ma'am."

"Cooper, I love the name."

"Yeah, me too. It's after Cooperstown."

She looked puzzled. She knew just about everyone in Cooperstown, and she was certain she didn't know these two. "You're not *from* Cooperstown, are you?"

"No, I only wish. You see, my dad and I love baseball, and when I was born, he chose that name. Actually, we never have even been to Cooperstown. This is our first time."

She couldn't help being captivated by this little guy. He was adorable.

"Oh, pardon my manners. My name is Lois, Lois Mason. And like the both of you, I love baseball too."

"Wow. A lady who loves baseball," Cooper mouthed to his dad.

"Mr. Anderson, I'm—"

"Please call me Blake."

"Very well, Blake. I'm terribly sorry about this, and I will make it right. I have some friends in the auto body business, and they will take care of everything… no cost to you or your friend, of course."

"That's great, but I only have a couple of days in Cooperstown, and I have to go back to the city and return the car on Sunday."

"No problem, Blake. I'll have the shop work overtime, and they will definitely have the car ready in time for you to leave."

"I guess your friends must like you a lot to do that kind of favor, especially this being the Legends Game weekend."

"Well, they are nice people, and I know I can count on them." Lois turned to Billy: "Billy, would you mind going inside and calling Tommy Love's garage and ask him to send a flatbed truck here to pick the Mini up right away."

"Yes, Ma'am, I'm on my way."

"Tell them I'll call them with the details."

Cooper carefully listening to the conversation and piped up: "But Dad, what about that ride around town, and lunch and ice cream?"

"Don't worry, Coop, we will figure something out."

"You won't have to," Lois added. "I'll take you both to lunch and give you the Cook's tour. I was pretty much raised here and know this town inside and out."

"But what about the ice cream?" He looked anxious.

"No problem, Cooper. I know where they make the best homemade ice cream in all of Cooperstown, maybe even the world, and I'm going to buy you a double dipper.

"Really? Cool ... thank you."

Lois Mason was also staying at the inn. But not as a guest; she was the owner. Her mansion overlooking the historical Otsego Lake was undergoing massive repairs from a serious water leak. The house had been uninhabitable for weeks. Lois was a youthful thirty-eight-year-old, who had never been married. There was a man, once a few years ago, who turned out to be more of a gold digger than a boyfriend. Lois had been deeply hurt by the experience. It had been a long relationship that ended badly with an aborted trip to the altar. The deep scars remained, and she had given up on the entire idea of marriage. She kept herself very busy managing the family foundation and its complex business enterprises and was content with her life and vocation, including managing the hundreds of employees who worked at the family foundation and its enterprises, which included multiple venues: hotels, restaurants, museums, and the Cooperstown Tourist Bureau.

Lois always remained grounded. She rejected a jet-set life like her sister chose and preferred a low-key existence. Her substantial wealth was inherited, but she worked hard and had no delusions of grandeur or feelings of entitlement, despite the fact that she actually inherited a substantial part of Cooperstown and was its most significant patron.

Lois piled the boys into her SUV as the flatbed truck pulled away with the Mini. "Lunch first, right?"

"Yes, I'm starving." Cooper moaned in the back seat.

"I have the perfect spot. It's a cute little restaurant on the corner of Main and Chestnut. It's called Sherry's"

The SUV pulled into one of the empty angular parking spaces on the side of the restaurant. Beautiful stone planters were methodically placed along the curbside, and the sweet scent of juniper evergreens filled the air.

"Pink?" Cooper yelled. "The restaurant is pink? Ugh. It's for girls."

"Calm down, Cooper," Blake said and glanced over his shoulder at his son. "Just because the restaurant is pink doesn't mean it's just for girls."

"Your dad is right. For reasons unknown, Mr. Shively painted the building pink years ago. Townsfolk figured he did it so it would stand out and tourists would flock there."

"Yeah, girl tourists," Cooper grumbled.

"Stop." Blake glared.

"I'll let you judge for yourself, Cooper." Lois opened the door to the restaurant and held it for the boys, and they entered.

Sherry's was a holdover from the 1930s. A large counter with a well-worn marble top flanked the room left to right. Red and chrome leatherette stools, one after another were neatly lined up and pushed under the well-worn counter.

The dining room was almost empty.

"Why isn't there anyone here?" Cooper asked.

"Probably because it's past lunchtime and close to dinner."

"Oh."

"Let's take a table," Lois suggested. "It will be more comfortable."

A husky waiter walked over to the table and with unusual courtesy, almost deference, greeted the group. "Good afternoon, Miss Mason. I'm so glad to have you visit our restaurant."

Blake and Cooper looked at each other.

"Thank you, Kenny. Now can you feed these hungry guys before they expire?"

The three chatted freely and enjoyed exchanging stories as their food came and they devoured their lunch. Lois was very knowledgeable about baseball, especially things related to Cooperstown and the Hall of Fame.

"So, I assume you gents are here for the big game tomorrow?"

"Yeah, we are. And I can't wait. It's been my dream to come here and now to be able to see the Legends Game … wowee!" Cooper downed the last of the French fries after liberally dipping them in the ketchup.

"Oh Cooper, I'm glad too."

"You know Miss Mason—"

"Call me Lois, dear."

"OK, Lois. Coming here is my birthday present."

"It's your birthday?"

"Yes, tomorrow. My dad and I have saved up for a long time and now we're here. I can hardly believe it." Cooper took a deep breath and continued. "Mr. Como, oh he's my dad's boss at the store, the baseball store where my dad works, well he, Mr. Como, told me that this was a lifetime experience. I'm not quite sure what that means, but Mr. Como is pretty smart, and if he says it is, well, it is."

Lois listened and smiled. She was captivated by this articulate little man who seemed so wise beyond his years. But even with all of the excitement she perceived a pair of little sad eyes and wondered.

"So, Blake, you work in a baseball store?"

"Well, not exactly."

"Yes, you do, Dad, don't lie. You work there almost every other night and on Saturdays and Sundays."

"Coop, I'm not lying. What I wanted to say, if you had let me finish, is that I work there part-time. But I'm a full-time teacher, vice-principal, and baseball coach at St. Timothy's in New York City."

"That's where I go, Lois. And besides being my dad, he's my coach."

"Not your teacher?"

"No. He teaches upper school, and I'm in lower school, third grade. You know he's really smart. He teaches math, and he went to Princeton. That's where a lot of smart people go. But even better, he is the best baseball coach, EVER!"

Lois grinned: "I'm sure your right. And I know Princeton *is* for smart people."

Blake called for the check, but Kenny waved him away. "No check, it's our pleasure."

Blake thought, *this surely is extraordinary hospitality.* Nonetheless, he reached into his pocket and took out a twenty-dollar bill. "Well, at least let me leave a tip." The threesome headed out the door, and Cooper couldn't wait for what came next.

CHAPTER FOURTEEN
LOOKING AROUND

"WELL, THE FOOD WAS PRETTY GOOD, BUT I STILL THINK A pink restaurant is for girls."

"Cooper, don't get all caught up with something so silly. The main thing was a nice lunch and that friendly man treated all of us. He was very generous."

Cooper turned so his dad couldn't see his face and mouthed to Lois: "It's for girls, ugh!"

Lois smiled the kind of smile that meant "your secret stays with me." "So, Cooper, are you ready for the tour, or will it be ice cream first?"

"Ice cream, of course. But I still want to see everything...."

"Right it is. Ice cream first! I know the best place in town, Pete's."

Pete's was the quintessential old-fashioned ice cream parlor right on the main street. Two bright red doors swung open and a pair of bells announced the arrival of customers.

"Holy cow, look at this place, Dad. They got way more than ice cream."

The walls were lined with shelves that displayed row after row of all kinds of candy. Penny candy, fancy candy, candy bars. A floor display was covered with Baby Ruth's, the iconic candy bar named for the daughter of President Grover Cleveland—even though everyone assumed it was after baseball legend Babe Ruth, and so they loved it in Cooperstown.

But what caught Cooper's attention was an entire wall from floor to ceiling covered with Topps bubble gum baseball cards ... hundreds of them. "Wow, wow, look at that, Dad. Mr. Como would faint if he could see this."

"Yeah, I bet he would." Blake laughed.

A skinny man in his fifties stood behind the soda fountain. "Hi, little fellow, my name is Harold, what's it going to be?"

"Ice cream, of course."

"Well, I certainly didn't think you came here to get your hair cut."

"Huh?" Cooper replied, failing to get the intended humor.

Seeing that the humor escaped Cooper, the clerk said: "Just a little joke. So, what flavor? We have thirty-nine of them. The list is up there." Harold pointed to a chalkboard over the fountain.

"Let's see." Cooper began reading them: "Triple-play Cherry Vanilla, You're Out Chocolate, Foul Sour Razzberry, Babe Ruth Strawberry..."

"That's enough, Coop." Blake grinned. "You don't have to read them all out loud, we'll be here all day. Just pick one."

It took a while, but Cooper settled on "Big League Bubble Gum."

"Here you go, fella. Big League Bubble Gum, double-dip."

Cooper's eyes were the size of saucers. "Oh, no, Dad, it's PINK!"

Lois was enjoying watching the two of them. It had been a while since she smiled so much in one day, and it felt so good.

Lois was pretty much alone in the world. Her parents had died years ago in a boating accident and left their vast fortune to her and her sister, Lenore. Lenore was a completely different person from Lois; everything Lenore was, Lois was not. Unrelentingly, Lenore insisted on the best of everything, and her parents had spoiled her beyond reason. She picked the fanciest boarding schools, barely finishing any of them, and never went to college because it interfered with her social life and European travel.

Lenore, who exceeded the definition of self-indulged and vain, was someone Lois had long ago decided the less she saw of her, the better off they both would be. After three husbands and an army of paramours, Lenore moved to Brussels, bought and completely refurbished a fourteenth-century chateau, filling it with fabulous antiques and studly men, one after each other.

Lois decided to remain in Cooperstown. She loved the place with its peaceful surroundings the calming lake, and most of all the genuine people who lived there. Over the years she had seen Cooperstown decline. Years ago, well before her time, the Great Depression had a major effect on the town's economy. But long after it was over, Cooperstown never seemed to bounce back. More recently recession added to the lack of development and prosperity. It pained Lois to see so many businesses decline or just disappear. Good and high-paying jobs were almost nonexistent, and the standard of living for other than the super-rich who summered there was low. Young people left as soon as they could for New York City and other places that afforded more opportunities.

It also pained Lois that the super-rich did little to help the town. They built massive "camps" that more resembled mansions, often bringing their artisans and builders with them, which deprived the locals of any opportunity to earn a decent living.

The Mason fortune was enormous. Winthrop Mason, Lois's grandfather, made his multimillions in manufacturing and later in real estate and oil. He was one of the first to invest in railroads early in the century. As part of New York's 400, the Masons followed the crowd and built a magnificent home overlooking Otsego Lake. It was this mansion Lois inherited and where she lived alone for many years. In February, when a pipe froze, major damage was done and Lois was forced to move to the Cooper Inn, where she occupied the entire left wing.

When she and Lenore inherited the vast fortune, it was divided in half. Lenore took hers and left town to enjoy the high life elsewhere. But Lois took another course. She wanted to spend her money wisely and, in a way, to help the people she had come to know and love. It was then that she formed a foundation that would have the sole purpose of restoring Cooperstown. Lois, unlike Lenore, finished college and was a business major. She understood economics and marketing and had a keen sense of investing.

Her first priority was to figure out a way to get Cooperstown self-sufficient. She knew that simply handing out money to people was not the answer, but what did work was giving people the tools to build their own destiny and financial future. Through the foundation, Lois immediately took action by buying up the neglected and dilapidated buildings along Main Street. She planned to rehab them making them appealing and authentic to the time of Cooperstown's inception. Once they were completed, one by one, she would either sell them to local entrepreneurs with liberal long-term financing or lease them to those who could not buy.

The Cooperstown Economic Council was started and headed by Lois, who put her money where her mouth was. In addition to rehabbing downtown, Lois directed the foundation to look into creating other tourist attractions and enterprises that could be funded and serve as a draw.

"Hey Lois, want a lick?" chimed in Cooper.

"No thanks, Cooper, but it does look awfully good, even though it's pink."

"Yeah, pink? But it tastes just like real bubble gum, honest."

"So, gentlemen, are you ready for that tour? There is lots to see."

"The Baseball Hall of Fame! Can we go now?"

Lois didn't want to disappoint Cooper, but she offered her advice. "Look, Cooper, it's getting late and you'll want to spend the whole day at the Hall. So why don't we look around at some of the other attractions, and tomorrow you will have lots of time, all day if you like, at the Hall of Fame."

"Sounds like a good plan to me, Coop."

Cooper looked disappointed but realized he was getting good, sound advice. "Well, OK, but I won't be able to sleep tonight thinking about it."

"Let's start with the Farmer's Museum. We can do a quick walkthrough, and if you like, we can come back again later. ... The Farmers Museum is one of our best-known attractions."

"Do farmers live there?"

"No, Cooper, they don't live there. It's just a place about them and many other things too."

"Oh, like what?"

"For one, it's the home of a really famous carousel. It was handmade, and it features New York State history. Way back in 1947, some fellow named Gerry Holzman and over a thousand volunteers all worked for years to hand-carved farm animals. You can take a ride on it if you like."

"You sure know a lot of good stuff, Lois."

"It took years to learn. And there's more. In the museum, there are lots of displays that you can interact with. You can even milk a cow!'

"A real cow?"

"No, but it looks pretty real and moos."

"Sounds like a lot of fun." Blake looked back at Cooper. "I read back in the room they have all kinds of shops, like a blacksmiths and general store, over two dozen buildings all over the place."

Lois's SUV pulled into the lot, and she parked in a staff parking space. "Follow me, boys; we can get in over there."

Lois passed the general admission entrance and walked towards an unmarked door. A uniformed groundskeeper noticed the threesome and rushed over to unlock the door.

"Good afternoon, Miss Mason."

"Oh, hello there, George. How's Mary and the kids?"

"Fine, they are all good. Thanks for asking. Will you be wanting the Governor's room unlocked? I can take care of it right now."

"No, George, we're just doing a quick walkthrough. But thanks."

"My pleasure, Ma'am."

The carousel was not operating when they stopped by to see it, but one of the workers spotted Lois.

"No problem, Miss Mason. I'll get the old contraption going in a second. Why don't you let that handsome young man get aboard and pick his favorite animal for the ride?"

The group walked around the complex for about an hour, and it was getting near sunset. "I have a brilliant idea, Cooper. I'm going to drive you around a bit more and show you some sites that we can visit later, and then we'll go over to the town dock and take a sunset cruise on the lake. I know you will like that. The water is beautiful, and you see all the lovely homes along the shore and the very famous Hotel Otsego."

Lois drove down the charming streets filled with late Victorian homes, many of which Lois had personally participated in their renovation. They went by Fenimore House, the ancestral residence of James Fenimore Cooper, whose father William was credited with founding the town centuries ago.

"Look at that house, Dad. It's like huge!"

"That's the place where famous author, James Fenimore Cooper, was raised and years later returned home to die. He authored countless books, most of them about the history of this area. *Leatherstocking Tales* is among his most famous works. If you like we can come back and visit. The inside is exquisite."

Lois drove towards the east side of the town. "That big building is our hospital, Basset Medical Center. It's a teaching hospital and closely affiliated with Columbia University. Each year famous New York City doctors come here and teach. They love getting out of the city for a while, and this facility was designed to attract them and their families. The town is very proud of the hospital; it is state-of-the-art."

Lois drove through town on her way to the lakeshore dock. Cooper couldn't help but notice the number of small baseball shops that dotted the street.

"You know what, Dad?"

"No, what, Coop?"

"I decided. When I grow up, I want to live here. I'll open a baseball shop and buy one of those fancy houses we saw."

"That sounds great. But, Coop, you'll have to sell a lot of cards to get one of those houses."

"Don't worry; I will."

A small crowd of tourists was waiting on the dock for the lake boat to depart. Blake couldn't help seeing how happy Cooper was. Lois noticed too and looked at Blake. "It's so nice to see him so happy. You are blessed, Blake."

*****

Cooper was up at the crack of dawn. He rushed to the lavatory, took a quick shower, and brushed his teeth. By 7:15, he was ready to go.

Blake heard the commotion but kept his eyes closed. He just wanted a couple more minutes of rest. When his alarm went off at 7:45, he opened his eyes, looked around the room, and saw Cooper patiently waiting, fully dressed, at the foot of the other bed.

"You're up. At last, come on, Dad. We got a lot to do. We need to go to the Hall of Fame."

"Coop, it doesn't open until nine. We have plenty of time, and I need some coffee first."

"What time does the baseball game start?" Cooper was referring to the annual Legends Game on Doubleday Field.

"Around two."

"Good, that will give us a lot of time at the Hall of Fame." Cooper searched around for his well-worn Yankee cap. "Dad, if we can fit it in the budget, maybe I can get a new cap and tell the guys it came from here."

"No problem, Bud. I think we can squeeze it in," Blake smiled and thought *he's a great kid, worrying about things like that.* It saddened Blake that Cooper even had to worry at all. In the old days, money was easy-come easy-go. But now, living on an educator's budget was a different story.

On the walk over to the Hall, Cooper stopped at almost every shop and priced Yankee caps. To his surprise, every shop charged exactly the same amount. In the end, he picked a store called "Play Ball" and charmed the owner into throwing in two packs of cards.

The tickets were for the third tier of the stadium, which sat just under ten-thousand fans. The boys hiked up the last flight of stairs and found their seats, which were a long distance away but faced the press box and VIP gallery.

"Hey, Dad," Cooper pointed out. "Look over there, in the box. Isn't that Lois?"

Blake strained to see. "Maybe, Coop. It's hard to be certain from this distance."

"It is, I'm sure. Look, she's got on the same jacket she had on yesterday, the blue one."

"Yeah, maybe. You know she works for the Foundation so she probably is there on official business."

"Lucky her, she can see everything."

"Perks of the job, I'd say."

The game was as exciting as Cooper expected. And now, Cooper thought it was time to eat. But where? Not that girly place again, he hoped.

CHAPTER FIFTEEN
LIKE POISONOUS SNAKES

After the game, Blake and Cooper walked down Main Street, looking for a place to eat. The restaurants were crowded, and long lines jutted out the front doors, so the dynamic duo opted to grab their third hot dog of the day at Newbery's, the local department store. Cooper browsed the aisles looking at all the stuff he didn't need. He checked out the Yankee hats, and sure enough, they were the same price there as everywhere else. He just couldn't quite figure out why.

As they were leaving the store, he spotted a bunch of vending machines. One had huge colorful bubblegum balls, "Dad, look at those gumballs! Gigantic! Have you got a quarter? I would like to get one."

Blake instinctively fished in his pocket for one but remembered he never carried them. He couldn't. Whenever he got quarters back in change, he either left them at the counter or asked the clerk for smaller coins. He knew it was ridiculous, but he couldn't help it.

Blake's body stiffened. "Sorry, Coop, I don't have any."

Cooper was more intelligent than that. He wasn't exactly sure what the thing with the quarters was, but he knew his father treated them like poisonous snakes. He asked once why, but his dad just brushed the question off.

Seeing that the mood had changed, Cooper suggested: "Dad, let's go back to the Inn and play catch. There is a nice green lawn there."

"Sure. We have all day tomorrow to do some more touring. But we have to be on the road by three. Hopefully, the car will be ready by then."

"Well, we can get up early and walk around."

"Not too early; places don't open until nine."

"OK, but we can always play a little more catch until they do."

Blake thought, *doesn't this kid ever get tired*? But then he remembered, he never did either, at least not tired of baseball.

Sunday morning was another perfect day. Warm, but not hot, clear, and blue skies. William at the front desk called to tell Blake that the Mini Cooper was parked out front and asked if he cared to check it out, to please do so. Cooper was the first one out the door to do a quality-control check.

"Looks like new to me, Dad."

"Sure does. We lucked out. It's a good thing that Lois had connections. Sam will be grateful that his car is being returned without damage."

Later, Blake suggested that they visit the Fenimore House and check out the art for which it was famous. Cooper had another idea: playing more catch. So, there was a compromise, a visit to the museum followed by some catch, lunch, and another walk through the Hall of Fame.

On the way to Fenimore's house, they passed the massive gates to the Hotel Otsego and a driveway that circled around to an enormous porte cochere, where uniformed doormen assisted the well-heeled guests.

"Dad, this place looks really fancy. Can we go take a look?"

"Why not. Looking doesn't cost anything, and I'd like to see it myself. Years ago, your mother and I went to a hotel like this in Kennebunkport, Maine." Blake thought those were the days. And then the never-ending sadness crept back into his consciousness about how a flip of the coin had been the beginning of a long and lonely existence for him and Cooper, how the two of them missed Amy in their own private ways. And worst of all, the nagging guilt that always came. If he had only agreed to Amy's insistence that she miss that interview and stay home with Cooper. History would have been different. Not because there would be no 9/11, but it would not have involved them.

"What's the matter, Dad? You look worried."

"Oh, no, I'm not worried; I was just thinking."

Cooper recognized the look now. It was the look that came when his dad thought about his mom. Cooper put his little arm around Blake's waist. "It's OK, Dad. Mom is here with us. I showed her the Hall of Fame already, and I know she is looking down right now."

Blake tried hard to smile and eventually forced one. He turned and wiped away a runaway tear.

"Let's pretend we are checking this hotel out for our next visit."

"Cool."

The lobby of the Hotel Otsego was a statement of understatement. Finished with pale blues and yellow tones, the lobby featured classic antiques. A brass Williamsburg chandelier towered over the seating area, and the walls were covered with subtle silk damask wallpaper and antique artwork.

Off the lobby were several sets of large French doors leading to a magical semi-circular covered porch. Twenty-foot high white columns reached the ceiling. In between the columns were gigantic hanging baskets filled with flowering plants and English ivy. But the most impressive thing was the unobstructed view of Lake Otsego. A long lush green lawn from the hotel to the shores of the lake was meticulously manicured. Flowering bushes and tall majestic oak trees dotted the landscape but did not obscure the view.

There were rows of white wooden rocking chairs set up for the guest to sit and enjoy the ambiance. The hotel was from another era when people took the time to appreciate the serenity of nature and the art of conversation. Blake could visualize genteel people sipping tea as they quietly rocked, occasionally chatting with their fellow guests.

"Can we sit here, Dad?"

"I don't see why not."

"Look, they rock." Cooper pushed back and forth, and the chair took off in a rocking frenzy.

"Well, hello there, gentlemen."

Blake looked up and saw Lois Mason. She was smartly dressed in a lovely blue-print outfit and a large brim hat.

"Lois!" screeched Cooper. "What are you doing here?"

"Following you! No, just kidding. Sometimes I go to church, and afterward I come here for a cup of coffee and their famous croissants. Have you had any yet?"

"No," Blake said. "Oh, they delivered the car, and it looks great."

"Perfect, I'm happy that they did a good job. And again, I'm sorry for the inconvenience."

Cooper interrupted: "Hey Lois, we saw you at the game yesterday. You were in the VIP box with all the bigshots."

"Yeah, that was me. I was working."

"Cooper and I were looking at this hotel; it's beautiful. You don't see structures like this much anymore, they're a time gone by."

"It's the crown jewel of Cooperstown, and we are all very proud of it. It had a head-to-toe renovation a couple of years ago which restored it to its former glory."

Blake looked at his watch. "We really have to get going. Cooper has planned the rest of the day, and time is flying."

"Lois, we have to go to some creepy art place. My dad thinks I might learn something, but I won't.

"How do you know that? Accidents happen," Lois joked.

"Na-ha."

"So, it's goodbye again. Thank you for being so kind, showing us around, and all that. We had a blast."

"I'm glad the car looks as good as new."

"You saw it?"

"Of course. I checked it out this morning before church; they did a great job."

"I'll say. They not only fixed the damage, but they also did a complete detailing. The car looks brand-new, inside and out."

"I'm pleased that you are pleased. And again, I'm so sorry for the inconvenience."

Lois took a moment to look at Blake and Cooper. She was really touched by them and, on some level, felt their pain. She had suffered catastrophic loss too and truly understood what loneliness was all about. She thought, *What a nice man, such a kind and loving father—and that kid, I could eat him up.*

Lois started to leave but turned back. "Blake, I really loved being with you and Cooper. Thanks for sharing this time with me." She smiled and Blake smiled back, not just a friendly one, but a warm, endearing smile that gave them both pause.

Blake took Lois's hand to shake, placing his other hand on top of hers. "Yeah, Lois. You were so kind to show us around. It was really nice." *Hmm,* he thought, *really, really nice.*

The Fenimore House was another amazing landmark. Even Cooper was impressed by the grandeur and graciousness of the mansion but totally disinterested in the priceless art.

After about an hour, Cooper whined: "Can we go now?"

Blake and Cooper headed back to the Hall of Fame.

They checked out every display again, walked through the corridors filled with busts of Hall of Fame recipients, and had their last hot dog at the concession stand.

"It's 2:30, Coop. We need to get back to the Inn and on the road."

"Dad, I don't want to go. Can we move here…*please.*"

"I wish. But come on, Coop, let's get going."

They arrived back at the Inn and settled their bill. "Coop, I asked William for some notepaper. I think it would be nice if you left a note for Lois. William said she was always around here, and he'll give it to her."

"Sure, Dad."

Cooper sat himself down at the bridge table in the corner of the lobby and composed his note:

Dear Lois,

Thank you for showing us around Cooperstown. You really know a lot about this place and are a lot of fun to be with. Pretty too.

And thank you for fixing Sam's car, even though it was your fault. But we're not mad at you for that. We are glad. Otherwise, we wouldn't have met you.

You are really a cool lady, and my dad thinks so too. He said maybe someday, my wish will come true and I will be living here selling baseball cards. Don't you think that sounds good? That is if I don't end up playing for the Yankees.

Love,

Cooper

Oh yeah, my dad says thanks too!

The ride home was just like the ride up. There was lots of trivia, some more license plate bingo, and a stop at the service center to fill up. By dinnertime, the boys returned to Brooklyn, returning Sam's car. As luck would have it, they found a parking spot only a few doors from Sam's apartment.

CHAPTER SIXTEEN
NOT COUNTING ON ANYTHING

THE SUMMER FLEW BY, AND SCHOOL BEGAN RIGHT AFTER Labor Day. Things at St. Tim's hadn't changed much; Mr. McHenry was up to his old miserable tricks. One thing after another, some very subtle, while others, more in Blake's face.

Blake often thanked God for Mr. Como and his part-time job. In a number of ways, the job was very important to him. The most obvious was that he needed the extra income. The money made a difference, allowing for some nights out now and then, among other things. He had had communications from various organizations regarding potential settlements for 9/11 victims' families, but he had read that such settlements take years and required dealing with lawyers and red tape, so consequently, he was not counting on anything. For all he knew, Cooper would be heading to college before the settlement came through. And besides, it would be ill-gotten gains, which was always troublesome to him. Another important thing was that the job provided a diversion from St. Tim's oppressive Mr. McHenry and the opportunity to be close to baseball. With Mr. Como and his growing friendship with

Rudy, their best customer, going to work wasn't like going to work at all. And the bonus was that Cooper loved everything about it. The store, Mr. Cooper, and Rudy, especially hearing their stories.

Rudy once told Blake that his father, and later he, ran a business, the rag business, as he called it. But Rudy was a little more than a rag merchant. And his baseball connections were a little more than getting some choice tickets by chance.

When Rudy started with his father, he was barely eighteen. As was with most immigrant families, the children rarely got educational opportunities and often went right into the workforce. If they were lucky, it would be in a small family business; if not, becoming a laborer or a service job was their lot. Rudy worked hard, but in every spare moment, he would steal off to watch baseball. At first, he would sneak into the ballpark, and later after befriending the security guards, he had free access. His secret was his mother's homemade chocolate babka cake. On Thursdays, she would bake double and triple batches from which Rudy would skim off a loaf or two and bring them to the guards. As a kid, Rudy was even more tenacious than Cooper and had no problem figuring out how to get what he wanted. Before long, the guards allowed Rudy to sit in the dugout during the games and kibitz with the players. Over time, Rudy made fast friendships with the players and was a regular at every game he could make.

Rudy had a good business sense. His father slaved making custom-made clothing for a fickle clientele, who often did not pay on time and complained constantly. Rudy learned the trade and concluded that the money lay in mass-producing something needed in quantity, which was undoubtedly not mid-priced custom-made suits. With a loan from his rich Uncle Burl, Rudy set up a small manufacturing shop on 7th Avenue, where most of the mass-produced off-the-rack clothing was made. His love for baseball led him to the idea of making baseball uniforms for kids. He researched and found that in the beginning, official MLB uniforms were primarily white, with the team's color added as trim. White turned out to be rather impractical on road trips since it soiled easily and washing facilities were scarce, so gray became the standard color.

In the 1970s Rudy realized that a new fabric was revolutionizing the ready-made market.

Synthetic fabrics had tremendous advantages over the old cotton or wool uniforms. It allowed an infinite variety of colors and printed logos and reduced maintenance costs: Synthetic fabrics were "wash and wear."

On a lark, Rudy made up a half dozen uniforms and brought them to the dugout for his player friends. They were an immediate hit. The players loved the craftsmanship and colors, and being made by a friend meant they were especially appealing. Soon, the uniforms caught Yankee management's eye, and they agreed to give Rudy the contract for next season. A whopping two hundred uniforms, making Rudy an official vendor and major contractor. When the team debuted in their new garb the fans loved them. Thousands of requests for team shirts were received by Yankee management. Rudy met all the players, and for those he especially liked, he would make a custom version of the uniform incorporating their specific requests. Rudy met the Yankees owner and hit it off, giving Rudy access to even more team events.

His company's reputation grew, and other MLB teams entered into contracts with his firm. By the end of the eighties, his company had contracts with five major league teams. Rudy became a baseball insider and could socialize with many of the greats. The company prospered, and Rudy was thrilled to be part of the baseball industry.

Rudy's biggest home run at financial success didn't come from baseball but the Metropolitan Transit Authority. The MTA held a contest to redesign their workers' uniforms. Hundreds of people entered, everyone from art students to professional outfitters, including Rudy. Three of the five MTA executives who were choosing the winning design also happened to be huge Yankee fans, and when they found out that Rudy was the official uniform provider for the team, it gave him an enormous advantage over the competition. In January 1990, Rudy signed a contract with the MTA to produce over seventy-two thousand uniforms for their thirty-four thousand employees.

Rudy was a quiet man and preferred to keep his success to himself as much as possible. He also was a man of meager needs and preferred spending time at the baseball shop with Mr. Como, Blake, and Cooper rather than hobnobbing on Park Avenue or gallivanting in European capitals or on other people's yachts.

Meanwhile, Blake spent a lot of time and effort keeping one ahead of Mr. McHenry. Off-season, he taught physical education but couldn't wait for baseball to start in the spring so he could coach the team. His days were filled with math, gym, and virtual dodgeball with Mr. McHenry. Early in November, McHenry gave Blake his latest challenge: to plan and run St. Tim's Christmas party for parents and donors.

"Come in, Anderson, we need to talk."

This was a very familiar command that usually came before being handed a hot potato.

"People liked what you did for the fundraiser, so I'm assigning you this year's parents-donors Christmas party. You know how important this is to the school, so you better not flub it up."

Blake nodded and continued to listen.

"As co-chair, I have asked Mrs. Ambrose-McAlister to serve, and she has graciously accepted."

Blake physically flinched. Not the dreaded Mrs. Ambrose-McAlister. Blake was intimately familiar with her. She had a pair of twins in Cooper's grade, Dean and Donald, and she was the most obnoxious, insatiable, snobby parent in the school. Hardly a week went by without an encounter with her. She would complain when "Donny-boy," as she called him, would get a lower grade than her "Deany." The fact that Donny-boy was not very bright and Deany was academically gifted didn't matter to her. Then there was the incident on the baseball team. Deany had a tantrum when he didn't make the first rung. The next day she demanded a meeting with Mr. McHenry and Blake.

*****

"Mr. McHenry. You do know who I am, don't you?"

"Of course, I know who you are, Mrs. Ambrose-McAlister."

"Of course, you do, but I'm saying that you know how important I am, especially to St. Tim's. My husband and I are probably your biggest donors, and we have had generations of family here at school."

"I'm well aware of that, Mrs. Ambrose-McAlister."

Blake was enjoying seeing McHenry in the hot seat. Now, perhaps, he knew what it was like to take it, not just dish it out.

"Well, we have a problem. You see, St. Tim's charming coach, our own lovely Mr. Anderson, has made a glaring mistake. He has not put my darling Deany in the first rung on the team. Poor Deany was devastated, and the other boys called him a loser. Nasty little trash, aren't they? Some of the first- rungers are even on scholarship. I just can't imagine picking one of those types over the cream of the crop here at St. Tim's."

Blake was almost nauseous listening to this insufferable snob carry-on. Even more intolerable was that her darling "Deany" was the least talented one on the team, and the kids hated him because all he did well was brag. He wore the most expensive sneakers at gym, had the latest and fanciest watch, and constantly flaunted it.

"Well, Mrs. Ambrose-McAlister, I can assure you coach calls it the way he sees it, but perhaps his vision, in this case, was a bit blurred."

Blake could see it coming....

McHenry turned to Blake. "Wouldn't you agree, Mr. Anderson?"

Blake cleared his throat, giving him a split second to formulate his response.

"We pick the first-rungers by capability, sportsmanship, and commitment to the pursuit of excellence."

Mrs. Ambrose-McAlister interrupted. "What the devil does that mean, and what does it have to do with my Deany?"

Blake knew he had to reduce this to the lowest common denominator, just like math. "It means we pick the ones who are the most talented and are willing to work really hard. And unfortunately, your Deany doesn't seem to love the sport the way his brother does. Surely, he has other talents we can develop—or he can work extra hard this year and make the first team next year."

"Mr. Anderson, please." McHenry jumped in. "I'm sure you are misstating the situation here."

"I would certainly hope, Mr. Anderson, that you can see your error. My Deany is a wonderful boy, and he is entitled to a position with the first-rungers."

"Entitled? First-runger positions are earned, not handed out. We can't teach our student body that being well-connected means you make a team over someone perhaps more talented. ."

"Anderson!" McHenry interrupted again. "I think that you should be mindful here; after all, this is a special situation with special people."

"Well, Mr. McHenry, it may be a special situation to you and Mrs. Ambrose-McAlister, but to me, the facts speak for themselves. Dean is not ready to be a first-runger, and until he develops as a player more, and as long as I'm the coach, he's not going to be a 'first-runger.'"

"Mr. McHenry, I can tell you right now that my husband isn't going to be happy about our Deany being excluded by this misguided coach. I am very familiar with Mr. Anderson. He also purposely gives Donny-boy lower grades than Deany just to cause friction in our family."

Blake shook his head. "I'm sorry, Mrs. Ambrose-McAlister, that's not at all the case. Donny does not do the work. I have encouraged him and worked with him, but he still doesn't turn in his homework. Both boys got what they earned."

McHenry saw this conversation was going in the wrong direction. "Mrs. Ambrose-McAlister, why don't you leave this with me. I'm certain we can get this resolved, Mr. Anderson and myself."

"Well, I certainly hope so. It would be a shame if the team didn't get those new uniforms, we were thinking about donating this spring, wouldn't it, Mr. Anderson?"

Blake remembered that he received a directive from McHenry three days after the meeting: "Put that kid in the first-rungers, now, no further discussion necessary."

Blake decided to take a position, be dammed the uniforms. He would ignore McHenry's directive. McHenry was furious but failed to intimidate Blake, who remained resolute. Mrs. Ambrose-McAlister kept true to her threat and did not donate a dime. To Blake's astonishment, new uniforms did materialize from an anonymous donor, identified only as RSC. This of course further infuriated McHenry.

*****

There was a voice message on Blake's phone. "The Christmas party date has been set, and Mrs. Ambrose-McAlister is raring to go. Give her a call; she is expecting one."

Working with this woman was more like receiving a sentence than a job. And, for the next four weeks, she proved it. Day after day and night after night Blake's phone would ring, and Mrs. Ambrose-McAlister would lecture him on what he was doing wrong or that she was unhappy with whatever it was at the moment.

In spite of the palpable antagonism and counter-productiveness, the party went off with only minor glitches.

The day after, Sam and Blake enjoyed coffee in the teachers' room.

"That was quite a party, Blake. You did a great job."

"Thanks, Sam, but many people helped and deserve credit."

"Yeah. But I thought it was incredibly presumptuous when that Mrs. Ambrose-McAlister got on stage and took all of the credit for herself. You would have thought she singlehandedly did the entire party."

"That's her. But thank God, it's over. I'm exhausted. It was like being in a shark tank: any moment could be your last."

"You did a great job, despite the odds."

"Thanks again. I can't wait for Christmas Break. I need some downtime and to get away from here. Between that woman and you know who, my nerves are shot."

"Got any plans?"

"No, Coop and I will do a tree this year, but it will be hard. He really misses his mother during holidays; she always made it special."

"And you, how are you doing, my friend?"

"A lot like Cooper. It's tough."

Blake and Cooper arrived home around five-thirty. They stopped at D'Agostino's and picked up a rotisserie chicken, mashed potatoes, asparagus, and two Dixie cups of chocolate ice cream for dessert. Cooper, as was his habit, grabbed the mail from the stainless-steel mailboxes in the front foyer and raced his dad up the three flights. Cooper usually won.

"Look, Dad, I got a letter."

"A letter? Who from?"

"I don't know." Cooper tore open the envelope and read it in disbelief. "You not going to believe it. Guess who it's from?"

"I have no idea. Only three people I know would send you a letter: Grandma, Mr. Como, or Rudy, and I'm not sure Rudy has our address."

Cooper, now on cloud nine, was jumping up and down and shrieked: "Wrong, wrong, wrong, it wasn't from any of them."

"Then who?"

"Lois Mason!"

"Lois Mason? How nice. Is it a Christmas card?"

"Sort of, but not really. It's a picture of Christmas in Cooperstown and a note inside. I'll read it to you:

> *Dear Cooper,*
>
> *I know you had so much fun when you were here in Cooperstown this summer. I did too, and I hope your dad also did.*
>
> *I'm writing to invite you both to enjoy Christmas in Cooperstown. The town goes all out, and there are lots of celebrations. The Hall of Fame has non-stop music and opens free of charge on Christmas Day. They give away lots of souvenirs and have a drawing to win some special baseball memorabilia from their archives.*
>
> *Come up the day before Christmas Eve. There is the official tree lighting and gala dance held at the Fenimore house, and I know you'll love it. They say Santa may show up too.*
>
> *So, let me know if you can spend the holidays in Cooperstown.*
>
> *Sincerely,*
>
> *Lois Mason.*

Can we go, Dad, please!"

"I don't know, Coop. The holidays are hectic, and it would be an expensive proposition."

"Please, Dad, I want to go. It could be my only Christmas present. Nothing else."

Blake thought about the money he had been putting away the last few months to make Christmas special. But it probably wasn't enough to finance a weekend.

"Coop, let Dad see what he can do. Maybe we can find an inexpensive place to stay. I'll have to rent a car, which could be pricy at that time of the year."

The two sat at the table eating their chicken. "Come on, Coop; you have to eat some of the asparagus."

"I hate them."

"Yeah, but they make you grow. I heard that asparagus are especially good for pitching arms. Lots of the pros eat them every day."

"I don't believe you. Dad, that's not true!"

"Well, it's what I heard, and who knows, it can't hurt to eat them just in case it is true. When I was at Princeton I had them three or four times a week, and boy, could I pitch."

Cooper looked at his father in disbelief but gobbled down the last spear, just in case the rumor was true, as his dad said.

As he chewed his chicken, Blake was trying to figure out how they could accept Lois's invitation. She didn't say and he didn't expect they would stay with her. That would be inappropriate anyway: an almost total stranger staying with an unmarried woman in a small town where everyone knows your business. No way! And besides, Lois didn't seem like the type looking for that kind of thing. After Cooper went to bed, Blake dug out a bunch of the Cooperstown brochures they had taken home with them; as he mulled them over, he spoke out loud to himself.

"Let's see. Well, this one is totally out." It was the Deluxe Hotel Otsego. "We couldn't afford the broom closet in that place."

The pile dwindled, and the next-to-last brochure was published by Cooperstown's Chamber of Commerce. Under the category of "affordable places to stay" were listed a dozen or so small inns and B&B's. There were no customer reviews, so picking a good one would be blind luck. As his finger worked its way down the listings, he stopped at one that caught his eye. The picture next to the description depicted a charming periwinkle blue Cape Cod-style house decked out in Christmas decorations. The property was covered with what looked-to-be newly fallen snow.

He read:

> *Gladys and Gus B&B, a nice place to say.*
>
> *Gladys and Gus graciously await every guest's arrival. Our charming B&B will be your home away from home. Our delightful rooms with lovely views of the surrounding hills provide privacy and comfort at very affordable rates. Just a few short blocks from downtown and the famous Baseball Hall of Fame, the B&B has everything you need for an enjoyable getaway. Complimentary breakfast and unlimited Chocolate Chip Cookies are graciously served to our guests, whom we consider more like family. Holidays at Gladys and Gus's are especially enjoyable. So, come, sit by our roaring fire and enjoy the charm and history of Cooperstown.*
>
> *Call for availability and reservations.*

Blake reread the part about affordability. "Privacy and comfort at a very affordable rate." He thought, *Well, maybe we can swing this.* Cooper would love to return to Cooperstown and being away for Christmas was a good idea. *We must make new memories, not sit here and wallow in the old ones.* Blake picked up the phone and dialed the number.

"Hello, Gladys and Gus's B&B; how can I help you?"

"Good evening. I hope it's not too late to call. My name is Blake Anderson."

"No, not at all. Even the chickens are still up…Ha-ha!"

"I was wondering if you had a room for two on December 22nd, out on the 25th?"

"Oh, young man," Gladys cooed. "I'm so sorry. We are full that weekend … filled up months ago."

"Yeah, I figured, last-minute Charlie here. Too bad, my nine-year-old wanted to come to Cooperstown for the holidays."

"Oh, you have family here? Anyone, we know?"

"No, not really. We do know Lois Mason; she was the one who invited us to come."

"Lois Mason? The Lois Mason who lives in Cooperstown, that one?"

"Yes, that's her."

Gladys scratched her chin and wondered: *This young fellow was invited to Cooperstown by none other than Lois Mason and wants to stay at Gladys and Gus's. How could that be? Any friend of Miss Mason must be rich, and besides, if she was inviting this Blake fellow here, why wouldn't she be putting him up in her mansion or one of the hotels she owns?* Gladys finally assumed this probably was just some guy name-dropping.

In the background, Blake could hear Gladys relating the conversation to someone else. He could hear her say, "He says Lois Mason invited him, and he needs a room to stay."

Blake continued to listen and heard a man say. “Well, if he is a friend of Miss Mason, we should accommodate him. What about the basement? We can put a nice bed there, and he could use the bathroom on the first floor.”

Blake interjected. “And about how much would that basement room be?”

Gladys asked Gus, “He wants to know how much for the basement room?”

“Tell him fifty-five dollars a night but remind him the bathroom is on the first floor.”

When Blake told Cooper that the trip was on, he replied to Lois’s invitation and told her they would be staying at Gladys and Gus’s B&B. Cooper was beside himself. Cooperstown, again! He couldn’t get over it. He remembered Lois’s note: Santa might be there. At his age, he was a little skeptical about Santa, but in his mind, the jury was still out on that matter. Maybe, he thought, just maybe....He’d have to wait and see.

CHAPTER SEVENTEEN
Not a Request, but an Order

"Only ten days, Blake, and we're out of here. I'm going to New Hampshire to see my folks. How about you?" Sam said as they sat in the teachers' room between classes.

"I can't wait either, Sam. I told you we got an invitation to go to Cooperstown for Christmas, and Cooper is on fire in anticipation."

"You did tell me, and Cooper told me eleven times. He said some nice lady invited you. Maybe a spark or something going on here...."

"Not with me, but if Cooper were ten years older, I'd be worried. No, she's a nice woman, but she's not for me, and besides, I'm not in the market."

Sam well knew that Blake was not in the market. He wondered if he ever would be. Although Sam never met Amy, he knew all about her. Cooper had told him lots of stories. Sam had picked up bits and pieces, so he understood that Blake still mourned. Blake, on one occasion, told him about the tragedy and the loss of her life. But Blake could never tell the bit about the coin toss. That was something he could never tell anyone. It just hurt too much.

"Just a few more days, and we can go. But I have a lot on my plate. McHenry has piled it high. The Christmas party, managing that with Mrs. Ambrose-McAlister was a living hell."

"I can only imagine."

"And then McHenry decided that all the lavatories need to be professionally steamed cleaned. Being, in his words, 'the toilet czar,' I have to supervise the job."

"What about Nick, the janitor? Why can't he do it? It's more his responsibility than yours."

"One would think so, but McHenry thinks Nick is too touchy to ask. He might get ticked off and quit. According to McHenry, it's harder to get a janitor than a Princeton graduate math teacher/coach."

"That guy is a clown show."

"No argument there."

School was to end on Thursday, December 22nd, and was in recess until after the New Year. Cooper was keeping a check-off calendar next to his advent one, and each morning he crossed off another day.

McHenry was well aware of Blake's plans through an army of snitches he encouraged. With maliciousness, McHenry concocted yet another scheme to make Blake miserable.

Over the school PA system, the announcement came: "Mr. Anderson, please report to the principal's office. Mr. McHenry needs to talk with you."

So far, it had not been a good day for Blake. Two of his math students got caught cheating, and one was Deany Ambrose-McAlister. He knew he'd have to call his mother, and that just turned his stomach. Mrs. Ambrose-McAlister had been making his life miserable for weeks while planning the Christmas event. There were times he considered calling Vinny, the butcher who lived on his street in Brooklyn, and ask him if he knew anyone who would rub Mrs. Ambrose-McAlister out. He feared that Vinny would actually know someone, so he never tempted himself by asking. On top of all that, Blake was in pain. He sprained his arm while playing catch with Cooper. It was the very arm where he sustained the injury that ended his chance for the major leagues. The two Advil he took weren't doing much to ease the pain or help with his uncommon irritability. He headed to the office for yet another dose of "McHenryism."

"Come in, Anderson. Don't sit; this won't take long." McHenry's dictatorial smug voice trumpeted what Blake knew was going to be just more bullshit.

"So, Anderson." McHenry looked almost gleeful. " You see, I got a call from Santi-a-Clean, and they have to move up the date."

"Santi-a-Clean? Who the hell are they?"

"They are the firm that has been hired to come in and sterilize and clean all the lavatories in the school, all thirty-two of them. And as 'toilet czar,'" McHenry wryly smiled, "You must be here to supervise the undertaking. They were scheduled for December 22nd at the end of the school day. But the company had a problem so they are now coming December 23rd, and you have to be here to supervise. Make sure they do a good job, and by the way, last time, you let them get away with the cheaper 'piss cakes' for the urinals. They promised the four-ounce ones, and we got the three-ounce ones, which don't last as long. So, you need to be here to ensure we get the larger ones this time. And see if they have peach-scented; they're the best."

Blake turned crimson. "What did you say? Did I hear you correctly? Supervise that we get higher-quality piss cakes? Are you kidding? I didn't go to Princeton to evaluate piss cakes. And besides. School ends on the 22nd, and Cooper and I have plans. We leave right after school closes for Cooperstown."

"Oh, isn't that a shame? You'll have to postpone your trip for a day. But this is important. Those sanitizer guys need keen supervision or they will do a lousy job. And then there is the bait and switch piss cakes situation."

The rage rose to a boiling point. *How dare this moron treat me like some janitor?* His disrespect and contempt were beyond tolerance. So much raced through Blake's mind. He had allowed himself to be treated like a third-class citizen by McHenry. He had worked his tail off and made the impossible happen. And by all measures, he had exceeded any reasonable man's expectations for an exemplary teacher, coach, and God damn toilet czar. The rage soon outweighed the reality that he needed this job; Cooper needed him to be around, St. Tim's was a great school, and Cooper was getting to go there without paying tuition. But how could he let this stand? The urge to tell this man off, maybe even punch him in the nose, was overwhelming. But, he thought, what would slugging him prove? And why risk getting arrested for assault? He took two deep breaths and calmly looked McHenry in the eye.

"No."

"No, what?" demanded McHenry.

"No, I won't supervise the steamers, no I will not quality control the piss cakes, no, I will not come in on the 23rd."

"Anderson, you don't seem to understand; this was not a request but an order. And you know as well as I do, orders must be followed, even by a tall, handsome Princeton graduate with $2000 suits."

And there it was, confirmation of why McHenry hated Blake so much. He just about said it out loud. Envy, pure and simple. Just Like Sam said, McHenry was green with envy.

Blake was done. Rather than engaging in a shouting match, he decided to do what bullies hate the most—to be laughed at. "Mr. McHenry," Blake laughed. "You don't understand, but let me make it clear. No, I'm not coming in on the 23rd. And that's final. And I'm not going to let some buffoon ruin my holiday." Blake headed towards the door.

"Just a minute, Anderson, you can't just walk out on me, I won't have it!"

"Oh, no? Watch me."

"If you walk out of this office, you're fired, through, finished!"

"Sorry, Mr. McHenry, you can't fire someone who just quit."

Blake walked into the outer office, bumping into Mrs. Lombardi, a parent who had overheard the entire to-do. From the corner of his eye, he saw Angie was already on the phone with Nick the janitor.

CHAPTER EIGHTEEN
Kinda Reminds Me of Mom

Thursday

The subway ride to Brooklyn was long and quiet. Cooper knew something happened between his father and Mr. McHenry but wasn't exactly sure what. He knew they didn't like each other, but that was nothing new. Mrs. Belinsky was there to check in with Cooper, and Blake headed to the shop for his afternoon shift. On the way, he became more and more worried. How would he support Cooper, and where would Coop go to school? What a mess he was in, and no one was there to help. He remembered his charmed life with Amy. How every day was a good one, and there were no worries, no money issues, and no Mr. McHenry's to muck his life up. If he wasn't so mad, he thought, he could almost cry.

The shop was packed with last-minute holiday shoppers. Mr. Como packed up purchases and rang the sales up on his ancient cash register, part of the store's charm. Blake assisted ladies who wanted to buy their husbands or grandkids collectibles for

Christmas. Framed pictures of all-stars and autographed baseball cards were the big sellers. The month of December had flown by, and he was curious about where Rudy had been since he hadn't seen him for a while.

At one point, the store was empty, and Blake had a moment to reflect...*What's next?*

He knew one thing for sure. He wasn't going to ruin Christmas for Cooper. He would put on a brave face, stiff upper lip, and worry about what was next when they came home from their trip. Fortunately, he saved up enough money for the Christmas trip but still had to be careful about spending.

"Hey, Blake, what's wrong with you? You look like the end of the world is at your doorstep."

"Nothing, Mr. Como, nothing." No, he was wrong about that. The end of the world had already been at his doorstep on that day in September.

"Look, Blake, I can handle the shop, why don't you take off? You have a long drive ahead of you, and you might as well get going. I'm good here."

Usually, Blake would turn down such an offer, knowing that Mr. Como could always use the help. But this night was different. He was done in from the turmoil with McHenry and worried sick about the ramifications of joblessness. He just wanted to run, so he took up the offer and agreed to leave early.

"You're right, Mr. Como. We do have a long drive. I'll take you up on your kindness."

"Great, now go, go. And Merry Christmas, Blake, and give my little buddy this little gift. Nothing big, just something I know

Cooper will love. Mr. Como handed Blake a bright red envelope. "And here, this one is for you, it will be useful on the trip."

"Oh, how kind of you, Mr. Como. You are the nicest man. And next year we will spend Christmas all together, I promise. Merry Christmas and thank you. Oh, if you see Rudy, wish him a Happy Hanukkah."

*****

Sam was using his car to visit his family, so Blake leased a holiday special. Blake took the subway to Murray Street where Hertz had a local pickup/drop off. The station clerk took Blake's information and filled out the forms. The manager called the garage jockey on the walkie-talkie, and the garbled reply came, which was only understandable by the Hertz clerk.

"Your rental package calls for an economy car, but I don't have any left. I do have a midsize, but it will cost you another $22.50 a day."

"No, I don't want to spend any more money."

The clerk clicked away on his computer, looked up, and said: "I have a Mini Cooper. They generally are a premium car; God knows why, they're so small. I guess it's still here because this time of the year, people want big cars. I can let you have it at the same price as the special holiday package."

"Mini Cooper? That's great. My son is named Cooper, and the last time we went on a trip, we had one. Where do I sign?"

Blake pulled the Mini up to the apartment and ran in to get Cooper. "Hey, bud, look what we got from Hertz."

"Another Cooper, a green one! Perfect for Christmas. Thanks, Dad, for getting it."

"Sometimes these things work out, Coop." Blake felt that maybe this was an omen of things to come. Maybe this little surprise would change the doldrums he felt. The boys packed the car; a large suitcase along with two small gifts that Blake had fought the crowds to pick up from Macy's layaway the day before last. Cooper carefully put the homemade Christmas card he drew for Lois in the back seat and a small box for his dad that he hadn't had time to wrap.

As they headed north, Blake couldn't remember if he had told Mr. Como that he would not be in on Monday, so when they stopped for gas, he called.

"Hello, Mr. Como, it's Blake."

"Hi Blake, is there a problem?"

"No, sir, I'm just calling to remind you that I will be out on Monday. We come home on Sunday, but I promised to take Cooper in to see the tree at Rockefeller Center that night. You're good with that, right?"

"Of course, my boy, you already told me that. Now, go, enjoy."

"Thanks, Mr. Como. I really need this time away. I've got a lot to sort out and being away with Coop for the holidays will help me get my bearings."

An hour or so after they had stopped for gas, the Mini Cooper pulled into the driveway, and Blake read the hand-painted sign: Gladys and Gus's B&B. A thick layer of snow covered the lawn, and just one parking space was left. Within a few minutes, they were checked into the basement "suite."

*****

The next morning: Friday

"Mr. Anderson, the phone is for you," Gladys called down to the basement.

Gus had outdone himself getting the room fitted out. After all, a friend of Lois Mason was, well, almost a celebrity, even though he was puzzled why such an important person would be staying in their basement.

Blake and Cooper were anxious to get dressed and go out in the cold crisp air. On the drive up, Cooper challenged his dad to a snowball fight, and Blake said, "You're on."

Gladys called down again, this time a little louder: "Mr. Anderson, phone call!"

Blake ran up to take the call in the kitchen. When he finished the call and went down to check to see if Cooper was dressed and ready.

"Who was it, Dad?"

"It was Lois."

Cooper's eyes lit up. "Lois? What did she say?"

"She's said she is tied up with work on Saturday, but she'll meet us at the Fenimore House around 7:30 P.M. A dance follows the tree lighting."

"Oh, no, you're not going to make me dance, are you?"

"I doubt it, and that goes for me too."

"Do we have to dress up?"

"Sort of. Lois said it would be nice if we could wear a jacket and tie. The dance is probably semi-formal. I suspected as much when I read her invitation, being that the event is at that fancy mansion. So, I brought your school blazer and a clean white button-down."

"Oh, Dad, it says St. Tim's on it. I'm going to look like a dweeb."

"No, you won't. And so what if St Tim's is on the jacket? Most kids would be proud to attend such a nice school; showing it off isn't bad. We'll be twins. I'm wearing a blue blazer too."

"The one Mom gave you?"

Blake didn't answer.

Gladys outdid herself for breakfast. She had enough food for an army. All the B&B's rooms were filled, so the table was crowded. A New Jersey couple scarfed down the last of the blueberry muffins and introduced themselves, mouths full. Another single woman in her sixties nodded hello. Gladys made the introduction.

"Meet Margret; she's a professional hooker."

Blake looked at Margret and then back at Gladys. "Oh." Margret had gray hair all done up in tight pin-curls and was so wrinkled it looked as if a good ironing would do her well.

Gladys busted out laughing. "She hooks rugs, dear, and weaves them with a hook. It's a craft from long ago. The museum is demonstrating the methods, and Margret is here to do it. The demonstration that is." Gladys roared.

Still reveling in the shock effect of her joke, Gladys asked Cooper: "What will it be, young man? Eggs, bacon, French toast, Captain Crunch?"

"I don't know; they all sound pretty good. My dad and I make breakfast on Sundays, and he makes the best pancakes."

Gladys immediately volunteered. "If you want pancakes, I can whip them up in a jiffy."

"Cooper," Blake interrupted, "Gladys has so many choices here; you don't need to have her make anything more."

"OK, I'll have the French toast, but I want to get going. There's a lot to see."

Gladys dished up a hefty portion of the delicious French Toast. Blake had some too. She smothered the toast with maple syrup and farm-fresh butter. "The maple syrup is made right here in Cooperstown. There's a farm shop just outside of the center, and they sell it right from their front porch."

"It's fabulous, Gladys."

"I'm glad you like it. I have a pantry full of it, and before you leave, I'm going to give you a bottle to take home. You'll remember Gus and me every time you use it."

Six inches of new snow had fallen that night. Everything was crisp and white and looked like a winter wonderland. The boys decided to walk to the Hall of Fame, just a few blocks away. En route they had that snowball fight they talked about.

The morning was spent at the Hall. Cooper read every wall plaque, trophy, and poster in the place. Around noon Blake told Cooper that some fresh air would be a good idea, and they could grab lunch too. The boys walked Main Street and passed charming little specialty shops between dozens of baseball ones. Cute names like The Smart Shop, Lucy's Essentials, The Church Mouse, and Coco in Cooperstown. Cooper soon found his favorite one. It was an old-fashioned candy store called "Don't Tell the Dentist." The moment he walked in he fell in love with the irresistible aroma of homemade chocolate. An enormous lady was standing in the front window rolling butter pecan fudge and cutting it into bite-size chunks for customers to sample. "Would you like to try, love?" The lady asked. The owner joined the group. He was a strapping chap in his twenties, and he explained that he loved candy, but his father was a dentist, hence the name. The boys left the shop with a small box of delectables to be saved until after lunch.

"Look, Coop, this place looks nice." Blake read the sign: "'The Hitching Post: Fine food and drink.' What do you think?"

"I don't know?"

"What don't you know?"

"I don't know what a hitching post is."

"Oh, I gotcha. Well, you see that statue of a boy holding out his hand with a ring? That's a hitching post; people rode horses in the days before cars. When they arrived at their destination, they would hitch the horse to a post so that it would not run away... hence the Hitching Post. It looks like this place took its name from that."

"Neat! Does everybody around here still ride horses or something?"

"I would think not so much anymore. Maybe sometimes. But it's more the idea of something from the past being used to add charm."

The boys entered the restaurant and ordered. After a great lunch, the waitress tempted them with dessert. "Try our home-made lemon chiffon pie. It's the house specialty made right here by the owner's wife."

"What do you say, Coop? Want to split a piece?"

"Yeah, I love lemons, especially to suck on. Can I get one too?"

"No!"

Blake finished the last bite of the most delicious pie he ever had. They paid the check and walked out into the cold but refreshing air. A large black SUV pulled into one of the parking slots and rolled down the window.

"Hello there, guys. How are you?"

Cooper's eyes lit up. "Lois, how cool to see you."

"And how cool to see you, Cooper, and you too, Blake. What are you boys up to?"

"We just finished lunch and the best pie I ever had."

"Lemon chiffon, right?"

"Right."

"It's my favorite too. But I can't have it too often. Not good for the waistline."

"Hey, Lois, do you know a good place where me and my dad can go sledding?"

"Sure, I have a friend with lots of land and sleds. You can go there."

"I want you to go too, Lois, please!"

Lois looked at Cooper and then at Blake, waiting to see his reaction to Cooper's invite.

"That would be great, Lois. Cooper and I would love that."

"Done deal. Let me make a call and make some arrangements. Put some warmer clothes on, and I'll pick you up at Gladys and Gus's in about forty-five minutes."

The ride from the B&B wasn't long. The SUV pulled into a long driveway, the entrance to some kind of farm settled in the hills just outside town.

"There are plenty of sleds in the barn at the edge of the property. We can use any of them."

Later, the dark afternoon clouds moved in, and a cold wind picked up.

"You see that structure over there, a few hundred feet from the old barn. It's a pavilion, and there's a fire pit inside, and we can warm up. Let me grab the basket in my car, I brought cocoa, and we can make smores."

By the time Lois returned from the car, Blake had the beginnings of a roaring fire going. The three sat close to the fire and each other. For the first time since he and McHenry had it out, Blake felt relaxed. The view from the pavilion was vast, one of the lake and the far-off hills. You could see a tall tower in the distance.

Cooper asked, "What's that tower over there?"

"That's Kingfisher Tower. It was built in 1876 by one of the wealthy summer residents from New York."

"It's really big, Lois."

"It is, Cooper. As I recall, it's more than sixty feet tall. It kind of looks like a miniature castle, eleventh- or twelve-century Gothic design. They say it was built of stones taken from the shores of the lake. And there are stained glass windows with heraldic shields in the center of each, just like the knights of the round table."

"Why did the rich guy build it? Did he live in it?"

"No, he didn't live in it. No one could; it wasn't built for that."

"Then why did he build it?"

"The story is that he built it just because he could. Maybe he just liked something to look at. You can see the tower for miles."

"Can you go into it?"

"Yes, and if you like, I'll take you someday."

Cooper looked across the frozen lake and at the Kingfisher Tower for a long time. He knew about King Arthur and the Roundtable;

his mom read stories to him about it, and his dad bought swords for them to play knights. Then an idea popped into his head.

"Lois, can you ice skate?"

"Yes, and I'm pretty good at it if I must say so myself."

"Then can the three of us go, on the lake, tomorrow, you, me, and Dad?"

"I told your dad, I'm pretty busy tomorrow. You know, making arrangements for the tree lighting and dance."

"Oh please, just for a little while."

Lois was worried. This little guy was just too irresistible, and he was stealing her heart. How could she say no to him? Mentally Lois sorted her schedule and figured possibly she could juggle some things around and make the time.

"OK, Cooper. Let's meet at the town dock at around three."

"Great, it's a date. I can't wait."

It was getting darker by the minute. The three came closer to the fire and talked a lot about nothing. It had been a long time since Blake felt the least bit interested in anyone other than Amy.

Cooper had wandered off to the nearby barn to look at the horses, leaving his dad and Lois alone in front of the fire. Lois looked at Blake and touched his face. She said: "Your face is getting red; maybe it's too cold; frostbite can sneak up on you out here. Should we go?"

"No, not just yet. Let's get closer to the fire, and we'll be fine."

As they moved closer, the glow of the fire was reflected in their eyes. Blake wondered if maybe this somewhat mysterious woman who seemed to love Cooper could be more than a friend.

Lois wondered too. When she looked a Blake, she saw a lot more than a handsome, charming, smart man. She saw a person who knew all about love, which he so abundantly shared with Cooper. She also saw a man with great loss. She wondered ... would he ever get beyond that?

Blake stood to put another log on the fire, which he poked with a large branch. When he sat down, he took Lois's hand, looked into her eyes, and was about to kiss the first person since Amy died. Just then, Cooper showed up.

"Hey, Dad, I gotta pee. Is it all right to do it in the snow?"

Flustered, Lois stood up. "I really have to run; I've got a million things to do."

Blake stretched out his hand. "Thank you, Lois; this has been really nice."

"Yes, it was really nice." She shook his hand; he held hers just a bit longer.

Lois drove the boys back to town because they wanted to walk around before having dinner. As she drove off, she said: "See you tomorrow and dress warmly."

"We will," Cooper promised.

Cooper turned to Blake. "You know, Dad, she kinda reminds me of Mom. Oh, I don't mean that she looks like Mom or anything. But she is always looking to take care of us and do things to make us happy."

Blake blinked away tears and changed the subject. "Let's walk down to the lake and see what we can see."

After dinner, the winds picked up even more. Snow flurries swirled around as the two briskly walked. Beautiful Victorian homes all decked out in tasteful Christmas decorations lined the street. From afar, Cooper heard Christmas music. In the distance, they saw a parade heading down Main Street. A marching brass band blasted out Christmas carols, and a vintage fire truck clad in evergreen roping transported none other than the man himself, Santa Claus. They ran towards the parade and waved as Santa tossed candy to the gleeful crowds of children. Blake thought that this slice of Americana was priceless. What a magical spot, and how lucky they were to be there.

"Dad, I'm getting cold. Can we go back?"

"Sure, Coop. I'm cold too. I'll bet Gladys will have some of those unlimited chocolate chip cookies and a vat of hot cocoa."

"Yummy. Let's hurry."

As they walked toward the B&B, Blake thought of dear Amy, how much she loved Christmas, and how she would have loved all of this. But knowing she wouldn't have another Christmas with them was heartbreaking. He was trying to keep it "light" for Cooper's sake, but it was very, very hard. Reality swept over Blake: he was jobless and lonely, going back to Brooklyn to certain uncertainty. His heart was heavy, and his future dim. Then a flick of joy cropped into his subconscious. There was Cooper. He was all the joy he needed. He was his reason to go on and make their way together. That would be enough for him.

*****

Saturday arrived bright and very early. Cooper sprang out of bed and raced to see what Gladys had made for breakfast. Down in the basement, Blake heard Cooper's scream. "You made them! Pancakes! Wow."

Cooper decided he wanted to return to the Hall of Fame again. He just couldn't get enough of it. Soon it came time to meet Lois down by the lake. They stopped at a local sports shop and rented skates and hiked down to the dock landing where they planned to meet Lois. When they arrived, they didn't see her so Blake approached a local man and started a conversation. He eventually asked if he knew Lois Mason and if he had seen her. They were all going ice skating on the lake.

"Lois Mason? Everyone knows who she is. But I don't know her personally. You see, I'm not in her social circle, not even in her league." Blake looked puzzled as the man continued.

"And you say she's meeting you here to go ice skating?"

"Yes, at three."

"That's curious, Lois Mason skating on the public lake. She has her own indoor hockey rink, and I doubt very much she'd be hanging around here to go skating."

"We are talking about the same person, aren't we? Lois Mason, she works for the Cooperstown Foundation."

The stranger laughed out loud. "Works for the Foundation? Look, mister, Lois Mason IS the foundation. In fact, she owns most of the town. Filthy rich, I'd say."

Blake was stunned. What the heck, he thought. Lois was clearly not leveling with him. All along, she put on the act that she was another hard-working person, like him trying just to get through. But no. She was a bloody heiress or something like that, wealthy, privileged.... Blake was beginning to realize why people around here treated her like some kind of royalty. This explained a lot.

Blake didn't know quite what to think. Lois seemed so regular, and she treated Cooper and him with such kindness and generosity. But, now knowing that she was a real "somebody" worried him. His small glimmer of attachment flickered. He, in many respects, could fit into her world. He had the right education, made a more than decent appearance, and even could talk the lingo. But he had left that world behind him, and he wondered if being with someone like Lois would thrust him back into the fast lane that he had come to devalue. He decided he needed some time to think this through.

"Hey, Coop, let's go. We need to go back to the room."

"But Dad, Lois is coming, and we are all going ice skating."

"No, we're not. Now, get moving."

Cooper knew by the look on his father's face and the tone of his voice that there was no room for negotiation.

Blake fumed as they walked to the B&B. He was completely bummed out. Was Lois making a fool of them? Was she another Mr. McHenry, playing around with his mind?

Gladys met them at the door with a message. She was acting as if some Hollywood celeb had called.

"Mr. Anderson, Miss Mason called and was wondering if she had misunderstood the plans about meeting you. She said she will see you at the Christmas tree lighting tonight as planned."

Blake eventually calmed down and decided to attend the tree lighting. It wouldn't be fair to Cooper to make him miss it. As for Lois, well, he'd just have to see.

*****

Fennimore House Dance

"Well, don't you two gentlemen look nice. I love the blazers. And look, Cooper's says St. Timothy's School. So cool."

"Thank you, Lois," Cooper replied.

"And this is for you." Lois leaned down and pinned a sprig of holly on Cooper's lapel. "And this one is for you, Blake."

"No, thanks, Lois."

Lois couldn't help but notice the change in Blake. He was at best frosty and at worst downright indifferent.

At eight, the tree was officially lit, and the society band began playing as the guests filed into the Fenimore House's ballroom. The room was elegantly decorated in gold and green. Huge vases of white hydrangea sprinkled with gold glitter were everywhere. Three antique crystal chandeliers were laced with ropes of princess pine and gold bows. This seventeenth-century mansion, home of the famous author, was the perfect venue for a gala.

Blake signaled Cooper to come over. "Coop, I think you were right; dancing isn't for either of us, so let's get out of here before some lady drags us out on that dance floor."

"Wow, yeah. Let's get out of here."

Blake was still fretting. He, on one level knew that he is just as accomplished as the next guy. But now, things were a little different. He was living the life of a teacher, not a "young Turk" and at the moment, he was jobless. Did he want to be some rich girl's boyfriend? He had college buddies who married for money, and it never worked out. No, not for him. But maybe things could change, and if they did, perhaps he could revisit this flirtation. Then he had a horrible thought—what if she thought he was a gold digger. Just after her for her money.

Still, he felt bad for being a little rude. He looked for Lois to tell her they were leaving, but she was the center of a circle of attention. A circle including women in furs and men in very expensive suits.

*****

Christmas morning came to Gladys and Gus's, bringing a light coat of fresh snow. The village looked magical. Gladys was up early to prepare a special Christmas breakfast: Belgian waffles covered with fresh fruit sprinkled with powdered sugar that looked like the fresh snow outside and smothered with locally harvested maple syrup. Gladys's grandmother's punch bowl was filled with homemade eggnog minus the spirits, set on the piano in the front room for all to enjoy. The full complement of guests sat and chatted like they were all old friends or family.

Once Gladys cleared the table with the able assistance of Gus, she invited everyone into the front room for a Christmas sing-along. Gus was conscripted into playing, and Gladys handed out songbooks she had picked up last year at the church. A roaring fire cast a special glow on the room as these total strangers melded as if they were all old friends or family. This was the part of innkeeping Gladys loved best.

After the singing, many guests excused themselves and were off to other commitments or plans. Gladys called Cooper over to the fire. "Mr. Cooper, there's a small something under our tree for you." Gladys pointed. "See it over there?"

Cooper opened the long package and was thrilled to find an authentic Hall of Fame baseball bat. "Wow, look at that. I can't wait to try it out." Cooper said. "Thank you so much, Gladys and Gus. You are the best." Cooper ran over and hugged them.

In their basement room, Blake gave Cooper the gifts from Macy's, which he loved, except for the socks and underwear. Cooper fished a small box out of his backpack and handed it to Blake. "Sorry, Dad, I didn't have time to wrap it up. Mrs. Belinsky took me shopping for it, and I paid for it with my own money, too."

Blake slowly opened the box and removed a simple acrylic frame. It had a miniature colorful Christmas ornament attached to one corner. Cooper had taken the picture of his mother from an old, discolored frame that sat on Blake's chest-of-drawers and placed it into this new one. Etched into the frame as an inscription: *Amy in Heaven.*

Blake struggled to hide his tears and, in the end, could not. He hugged his little man, thrilled to have him in his life. "It's beautiful; thank you, Cooper. I love it."

"I'm so happy that you do, Dad. Now Mommy will always spend every Christmas with us, even if only in the picture."

"Well, Bud, it's time to pack up and say goodbye to Gladys and Gus. We have a long ride."

Cooper gathered his things and discovered that he had neglected to give Lois the Christmas card he had made for her. "Hey, Dad. Look, I forgot to give Lois my card. Can we go see her?"

"No, I don't think so. You know what? We can drop it off at the Baseball Hall of Fame. Everyone there knows her, and they will make sure she gets it."

"Great idea, because now I can walk through it one more time before we leave. I forgot to look at something."

"How could you? You were there for hours and looked at everything."

"'Cause I just did. Come on, let's get going."

CHAPTER NINETEEN
Darkest before the Dawn

After the holidays, Blake began to look for a job in earnest. He had two career paths: Wall Street and education. Mid-year was always a hard time finding a teacher's job. Most schools' budgets were fixed during the summer for the upcoming fall term. He chased down a couple of leads that had part-time positions but were at schools that did not offer free tuition for Cooper. Luckily with Stu's help, St. Tim's agreed to keep Cooper on for the rest of the year. However, he was required to sign a note promising to pay the half-term tuition back.

Blake's confrontation with Mr. McHenry did not go without notice. Mrs. Lombardi, one of the parents, overhead the episode and was quite upset. She was one of the board members who particularly liked Blake, and she was always a bit put off with McHenry's puffed-up persona. She decided to bring the situation to the attention of the board and at the very least demand a full explanation why such a popular and effective teacher and coach would feel resigning was his only option. She knew Principal McHenry was popular with the board. Years ago, when private schools were struggling to survive, reeling from the downturn in the economy and popularity of some newer institutions with a different approach to education, McHenry had virtually single-handedly saved the school from going under by touting and effectively marketing the "old school" classical approach reinforcing traditions that were being rejected or devalued by the more liberal institutions. Simple things like requiring boys to wear ties and jackets while attending classes, regular attendance of chapel, after-school one-on-one mentoring with teachers, and a "decent" haircut! This made St. Tim's an attractive alternative for parents who rejected the avant-garde approach and sought a more old-school approach toward education. The formula worked, and St. Tim's became the go-to school for future ladies and gentlemen. This track record, coupled with McHenry's strong personality and long tenure sort of lionized him.

For Blake, the Wall Street option was probably still there. He knew he could reach out to old friends and contacts on the street. He had been successful at Morgan and given the circumstances under which he left, concessions were often being made to accommodate survivors, so getting a new position would not be as difficult as he previously thought. But he realized going back to the rat race on Wall Street wouldn't work. It meant long, grueling hours away from Cooper, leaving him in the care of strangers. No, Cooper lost his mother, but he certainly wasn't going to have an absentee father. Wall Street was out of the question. He needed a job that worked for both of them.

That left education. His experience at St. Tim's demonstrated his abilities, but the way he left could be problematic. Getting a favorable reference out of McHenry would be unrealistic.

Perhaps Stu could help? Blake would just wait and see how it all would play out.

For now, it was Mr. Como's shop. He worked as many hours as possible. He loved the work, especially the customers, but the money was barely enough. One day he got wondering about his old friend Rudy.

"Mr. Como, have you seen Rudy? Has he been in?"

"No, Blake, I haven't seen him since before Christmas, maybe around Thanksgiving. He left some things here on consignment but never came by to pick up the money."

"Do you know where he lives?"

"Not really, but I recall him talking about going somewhere in Florida for the winter. Not sure when or where though."

"Well, if he should stop by when I'm not here, be sure to ask him to get in touch. Cooper and I miss the old guy."

Bills mounted, and Blake was falling behind in the rent. Cooper needed some dental care that was not covered by insurance, which added to the mounting bills. Just before Easter, things were becoming desperate. There were no jobs in the offering, and things seemed grim.

Mr. Como worried about Blake. He was losing weight. And carried a heaviness on his shoulders even more than before.

At night while lying in bed waiting for sleep to find him, Blake would talk to Amy. "Babe, I hope you're listening. Cooper swears you can hear him when he talks to your picture. I hope he's right."

Blake rolled over and stared at the empty side of the bed, the spot where he would often watch Amy peacefully sleeping. "It's getting really rough, and I'm feeling so low and lost." Blake rolled over again, this time facing the blank peeling wall on his side of the bed. "I remember you used to say 'it's always the darkest before the dawn.' Well, babe, I hope you're right because things really couldn't get much darker."... Could they?

CHAPTER TWENTY
LIKE A SPEEDING BULLET

BASEBALL SEASON WAS OPEN. THE YANKEES WERE PREDICTED to have a banner year, and people were already talking World Series. Blake, still drudging it out at Mr. Como's, was now being considered for a teaching job at another private school in the city, called Winslow Academy. All the interviews went well, and it was now a waiting game. Maybe Amy was right, it is always darkest before the dawn; things might be working out.

With some serious overtime and belt-tightening, Blake got caught up on his rent, but outstanding bills still needed to be addressed, and a little more dental work for Cooper was looming. Mr. Como had been a wonderful friend and a generous employer. He understood Blake's situation and tried to help make things easier for them. On a rainy Wednesday, Mr. Como surprised Blake.

"Blake, you know, from time to time, I get complimentary tickets to the game. So, a pair of these came in, and I thought you and Cooper would like to go."

"Wow, but don't you want to?"

"Nah, I have seen many games in my life and know how much Cooper loves the Yankees. This is a doubleheader on Saturday, so it will make a great day." Mr. Como knew there weren't a lot of extras for the boys and giving them tickets was something that would break up the doldrums.

On Saturday, Cooper woke early and dashed into Blake's room holding a steaming cup of coffee. "Wake up, Dad, we have to get going.... the game...remember?"

Blake opened his eyes to the delight of seeing his handsome son, bright-eyed and bushy-tailed holding this favorite mug—the one that said "Number-One Dad."

"Coop, it's only 6:45."

"I know, but we got a lot to do. First, we have to pick up the apartment, then the laundromat, ugh, and that dryer."

"Don't worry, sport, we'll make the opening pitch in plenty of time. Now, come here and give your dad a big hug; I need it."

Cooper jumped into bed and snuggled next to his dad. He remembered when his mom was alive and how the three of them would cuddle. On some level, Cooper understood that it was just the two of them against the world. And, without question, he knew his dad was there for him and could be counted on unconditionally. This was a lot of understanding for a kid, but somehow, Cooper embraced it. Not having a mother made having such a great dad even more important; Cooper knew that for sure.

"OK, hug time over," Blake announced as he sat up.

The two raced around the apartment, picking up the odd dirty glass and ready-for-the-washer tee shirts. It didn't take long, and the place was "picked up." However, in Mrs. Belinsky's estimation, their handiwork was never quite perfection and the apartment always was ready for a good cleaning, which she did for them occasionally, free of charge.

The laundromat was hated by Blake not just because it was so boring. It wasn't the pre-spotting, the mountains of folding, the slow, noisy dryer, or the sometimes-creepy customers; it was something far more symbolic than physical. It was the quarters. Each machine required the insertion of four or six quarters. The same kind of coin he had flipped with Amy the day she went to work and never came home. Blake had come to giving Cooper bills and having him change them for the quarters and letting him feed the machines.

Chores done, the boys rode the subway to the Bronx, enjoying a rousing round of baseball trivia. Blake was amazed at how much knowledge Cooper had acquired over the years.

"Dad, after the game, could we go to Mr. Como's store and look around?"

"Sure, Coop. You will be able to thank him for these tickets. They were a wonderful gift."

The seats were incredible, first-row centerfield. Blake wondered how the heck Mr. Como got such great tickets.

It was the second inning when a Yankee batter connected, hitting a long line drive. The ball skipped by various barriers and shot into the stands, striking Cooper squarely in the head like a speeding bullet. Blake couldn't believe his eyes and was stunned. Within moments, medics rushed to the scene, followed by a legion of more medics all surrounding the unconscious Cooper. Blake watched speechlessly, too shocked to react.

The injury was serious. A medevac helicopter rushed Cooper and Blake to the rooftop of Columbia Presbyterian Hospital, where an alerted triage team awaited. Cooper regained consciousness in the helicopter and looked up into his father's worried, tearful eyes. He could hear him say. "Don't worry, Coop; they're going to fix you up."

Cooper, could tell by the look on his father's face that things were not good. Fear gripped him, and he was petrified. Maybe he was going to die! But then, a sort of calmness enveloped his small body. Something people say happens when you are near death. Cooper stared back at his dad and spoke ever so softly.

"Don't worry about me, Daddy, it's going to be OK. I'll be seeing Mommy, and she'll take good care of me, just like you have. I'll say hi for you. I promise you'll be all right, Daddy, just like you always promised me; that I'd be all right."

Blake couldn't bear hearing his little man saying this and was reduced to inconsolable tears. A female medic put her arms around him and comforted him. His mind raced; how could this happen, my boy being snatched away from me? He had been cheated by death when Amy was taken from him, and now maybe again when his beloved Cooper, the only person in the world that gave his life meaning and purpose, might be taken too. Blake clutched Cooper's little hand, the one that he wore his favorite baseball glove on, the one that, as a child, he clasped as they would skip down the street. Blake said, "You're going to be OK, Coop." But he stopped short of saying I promise because he couldn't.

Cooper mouthed, "I know, Dad, and I love you." Then Cooper sunk back into unconsciousness.

A couple of excruciating hours in the waiting room took its toll on Blake. He couldn't sit still or even think straight. He dreaded every minute that ticked by, not knowing what was happening.

"Hello, Mr. Anderson?"

"Yes, that's me. How is Cooper?"

"I'm Dr. Calagaro, part of the team evaluating Cooper. We have put him into a medically induced coma. This is common with head injuries because it allows the brain to settle down, etc."

"Go on, tell me."

"The injury is serious, very serious. Your son has sustained a severe head injury resulting in critical brain trauma. We need time now to see if the cranial bleeding subsides."

"And if it doesn't, Doctor?"

"Well, that would indicate surgery. Mr. Anderson, may I be frank with you?"

"Yes, yes, of course."

"Cooper is in critical condition. His chances are unknown, but he is young and healthy, which counts for a lot. The next few hours will tell the story. All we can do is wait…and see. The hospital has a special area set aside for loved ones to wait. May I have the nurse take you there? It's just a little away from the ICU, where Cooper is."

"Can I see him?"

"In a little while. He's hooked up to a lot of equipment but let us get him sorted and then…perhaps."

"Thank you, Doctor."

The special area was a lovely room with a view of the East River. Someone had put a lot of thought into it. The colors were cool and soothing, and the furniture soft and welcoming. There was a small refreshment bar with coffee and bottles of water, and a TV on the wall with the sound turned down. A table with three chairs faced the view and on an end table was a telephone.

The room was just big enough to pace, and that's what Blake did. Eventually, he was so fatigued that he sat on the comfy sofa and closed his eyes.

"Mr. Anderson."

Blake opened his eyes to see a pleasant-looking nurse standing at the door.

"Yes, I'm Anderson."

"If you would like to see your son now, I can take you there."

"Yes, of course."

"He's still unconscious but resting peacefully. Don't be alarmed; his head is bandaged, and there are several IVs. Are you going to be OK with that?"

Blake swallowed hard, nodded, and followed the nurse down the corridor.

"In here, sir."

CHAPTER TWENTY-ONE

IF MUHAMMAD CAN'T COME ...

THE HOURS FLEW BY SINCE THE ACCIDENT, AND BLAKE returned to the special room and impatiently waited. A soft knock on the door drew his attention, and two physicians entered.

"Good morning, Mr. Anderson. I'm Dr. Lawrence, and this is Dr. Levy. The internal bleeding has subsided but not ceased, and all our tests indicated that surgery is the only option. His condition has not improved and, in fact, is getting slightly worse. As we initially suspected, your son requires surgery."

Blake paled and put his hand to his mouth. "Oh, no!"

"The operation is tough and would require a rather extended recovery time, weeks perhaps, in hospitalization."

Blake couldn't believe it, but the news kept getting worse and worse.

"The team of physicians attending your son just finished meeting to evaluate the surgery option. Unfortunately, none of the physicians on staff feel comfortable performing such a delicate and risky procedure."

Blake interrupted: "What do you mean? Does no one want to operate on Cooper? You're just going to let him die?"

"No, Mr. Anderson, that's not what we are saying. Please sit down; let me explain. We are saying that there is really only one doctor, a pediatric neurosurgeon, Dr. Ivin Moskowitz, who is eminently qualified to do this complex and delicate surgery, but he is currently not here. He's on a two-week teaching/lecturing commitment and is not due back to Columbia for another seven days."

"So, does Cooper have to wait for this doctor? Can't he fly back to perform an important surgery?"

"I'm sorry that isn't possible. As part of his teaching commitment is doing a pro bono surgery on a child with a complex brain tumor. He can't be here and there at the same time. Mr. Anderson, we are working on an alternative to that. The chief of staff is trying to locate another doctor who possibly would take on the procedure. Be assured we will keep you advised as soon as we have a resolution."

"But will another doctor be as qualified as this doctor? What's his name?"

"His name is Moskowitz, Ivin Moskowitz. With respect to another doctor's qualifications for this type of surgery, I can't say. But clearly, Moskowitz is the leader in the field."

Blake sank back into the sofa as the two white coats left the room. He felt helpless. He needed to talk to someone who could help. "Stu … I'll call him; he'll know what to do." Blake picked up the phone and made the call.

"Hello, Stu, it's Blake. There's been an accident, and I need your help."

Blake was right. Stu did know what to do. He said, "Wherever this Dr. Moskowitz is, we'll bring Cooper. If Muhammad can't come to the mountain, we'll get the mountain to Muhammad."

Stu had connections and used them well. He first called his brother-in-law, who had a Hampton summer house next door to one of the major investors in the Yankees. Within a couple of hours, Cooper and Blake were aboard the Yankee's team jet on its way to Columbia's teaching hospital, Basset Medical Center, located in Cooperstown, New York, where Dr. Moskowitz awaited.

The sleek jet plane landed on a private runway owned by the Mason family. Blake held the still-unconscious Cooper's hand the entire way, occasionally moving to allow the flight doctors to check Cooper's vitals and adjust the apparatus. He thought, God if only Cooper could see this, being on the Yankee team plane. Suddenly a dark thought crossed his mind. *What irony, baseball, the thing that Cooper loved most in life, might be the thing that would now take it from him.*

An ambulance was on the tarmac waiting as the still-comatose Cooper was whisked off the plane on a gurney. His bewildered father followed the entourage of scrub-clad people. The airport was only a few miles from the hospital, and when the ambulance arrived, another team of physicians had the operating theater ready to go. Doctor Moskowitz had all of the X-rays and scans sent ahead and was well-versed in the situation. Moskowitz did not take the time to come and talk with Blake. He wanted to get the surgery done immediately.

It was a long complicated surgery; it took hours. The waiting was excruciating for Blake, who, by now, was completely exhausted, running on empty. Around four in the morning, Dr. Moskowitz and a nurse entered the small area where Blake waited.

"Good morning, Mr. Anderson. I'm Dr. Moskowitz"

Blake rose and shook his hand. He was surprised, expecting an older man, one perhaps huskier and with broader shoulders. Someone a bit more mature and masterful looking. But Dr. Moskowitz was not any of that. He was surprisingly young, a handsome baby-faced man no more than thirty-five or -six. He was slender, fair-haired, and not very tall. But the real surprise was that this apparently famous young doctor was compassionate.

Dr. Moskowitz sat and asked Blake to sit beside him. He smiled, a warm, comforting one.

Blake couldn't stand the suspense: "How is Cooper? Is he going to be all right?"

"I believe the surgery was a success. But it's too early to tell the outcome. It was a very intricate and delicate operation." The doctor took Blake's hand. "Mr. Anderson, I have a boy about Cooper's age, and believe me I know how hard this must be. But I want to assure you we did our very best, and I can say I'm guardedly optimistic."

Blake related to the kindness and compassion of this young doctor. "Thank you, Doctor. But what can I expect?"

"Cooper will be in ICU for a while, maybe a week or so. Then he will need bed rest for another week or more. He must be kept quiet and not have a lot of physical activity. Some improvement might show early on, but a total recovery could take some time."

"How much time?"

"Only God knows."

Blake scoffed to himself, *God.* He long ago gave up on that idea. After Amy and now Cooper, faith was hard for him to accept.

"Mr. Anderson, nothing more is going to happen now. Go home and get some rest. Come back in the morning, and we'll know more."

"I can't leave."

"Sir, please trust me; nothing more will happen tonight. Go home, get some rest."

Blake looked into the doctor's eyes and could tell he was telling the truth.

The doctor was right. He needed to get some rest and clean up. He hadn't brought a thing with him and was in desperate need of a change of clothes and a hot shower, so he called Gladys and Gus.

Less than ten minutes later, Gus's old Ford truck was out front of the hospital to pick up Blake. Gladys was home, making up their best room, one with a private bathroom on the top floor for Blake. Gus called her and said Blake didn't have any clothes with him, so Gladys rummaged around her attic and found a suitcase some guests left and never claimed. It had several changes of clothes and an unused toilet kit from Swissair. By the time Gus and Blake arrived, Gladys had a second batch of chocolate chip cookies in the oven and a fresh pot of coffee brewing.

"Blake, I'm so sorry."

Blake couldn't maintain his composure for another second and he sunk into Gladys's comforting arms and wept. She patted his back gently and let this desperately scared man let it all out. She knew from experience that a good cry, even for a man, was sometimes the only thing that helped.

*****

The day after the accident.

Mr. Como opened his shop around ten in the morning. He wasn't very busy but usually never was until later in the afternoon, and early evening, so he hung the "Back in Five" sign on the door and popped next door for a cup of Aunt Bea's java. Bea was busily attending to a late breakfast crowd and waved to Mr. Como as in walked into the luncheonette. "Take a stool, Mr. C. I'll be right with you. And in her typical German efficiency had a steaming mug of java in front of him before he was fully seated.

"What's new?"

"Not much, Bea. The store is a bit slow lately."

"Have you seen Rudy around? He hasn't been in for a while."

"No, I haven't seen him, but sometimes he takes off for a few days, or even weeks, especially during the winter months. He'll probably be around in a few days, I'd guess. How's the strudel today?"

"How's the strudel, he asks? It's the same as it is every time I make it, delicious!"

"Oh yeah. So, how about a piece? But cut it in half. I'll have the rest of it after lunch."

Bea gave him the "look," grunted, and cut the pastry in half. "I'll wrap the other piece up for you, no charge!" Bea busted. "How about Blake? Where is he?"

"Not sure, he and Cooper went to a doubleheader yesterday, and Blake had today off, so I guess they are home resting up from a late night at the park."

"Hmm. I miss him and that little tiger of his. What a cutie pie. I'm going to make him some ginger snaps tomorrow. It's one of his favorites. I'll frost them like baseballs and put the NY Yankee logo on them."

As the two were chatting a young man caring a carton entered the luncheonette. "Excuse me, Ma'am, but I went next door and nobody is there. Do you know where I can find a Mr. Blake Anderson from Field of Dreams?"

Bea looked at the handsome young man's uniform and read the embroidered patch on his breast pocket: Brinks Bonded Courier Service, followed by a name tag: Walter Draper. She noticed he was armed with a pistol securely snapped in a holster. "Yeah, I know Blake Anderson, what's it to you?"

"Oh really, Ma'am, do you know where he is?"

"Well, he works next-door, but today is his day off." Bea paused. "But this old coot is his boss, Mr. Como."

The polite young courier approached Mr. Como. "Excuse me, sir, but I have a package for Mr. Blake Anderson. It requires a signature. Would you be willing to accept the package for Mr. Anderson, sir?"

"Sure, kid, why not? He'll be back to work tomorrow or the next day."

"Great, sir. Thank you. Can you provide me with some form of ID so we have a record of who received the package?"

Mr. Como looked puzzled and then a bit annoyed. "ID? Are you kidding me?"

"No, sir. It's just procedure. When a package like this is delivered, proof of delivery along with an ID verification is required."

Reluctantly, Mr. Como reached into his pocket and pulled out a thick, well-worn leather wallet with two elastic bands wrapped around it. He fished out his driver's license and showed it to the courier. "Here you go, young man."

Walter took the license and examined it carefully. "Thank you, sir, but it seems that your license is expired."

Mr. Como grabbed the license out of the courier's hand and looked at it. "Holy crap, it is. Well, you see I don't drive much anymore. I don't even have a car...."

Walter looked at the license again. "Do you have any other identification, sir?"

Now really annoyed, Como said: "Look kid, that's it. Take it or leave it. I don't even know what the hell the package is. In fact, you can take the package and send it back to whomever."

The young courier paused and then said: "Well, the purpose of the ID is to make sure the person who received the package is who he claims to be. I suppose it's irrelevant that your ID is expired."

Bea who was taking this all in chimed in: "And I can vouch for this guy. He is who he says."

"Very well, sir, please sign here."

Mr. Como couldn't resist and didn't save the second half of his strudel, so he unwrapped it and washed it down with another cup of coffee. "Gotta run, Bea, I'll see you tomorrow." As he headed towards the door, Bea waved, and yelled: "Hey, dummkopf, you forgot Blake's package. I tell you, you men would forget your heads if they weren't attached."

"Oh, yeah. Thanks!"

When Mr. Como returned to the shop, he switched the sign on the door back to "open" and looked at the box. It was the size of a file folder and weighed about two pounds. He read the return address: Donavan, Donavan and Coil LLP. "Lawyers." He thought, *I hope Blake isn't in trouble. I'll put the box in the back for him.*

As Mr. Como returned to the shop the phone was ringing: "Hello, Field of Dreams, can I help you?"

At the other end of the phone, there was a few seconds of silence. "Hello, hello, is anyone there?" asked Mr. Como.

In a barely recognizable voice, a choked-up Blake spoke. "Mr. Como, it's Blake." He decided to call before the news about Cooper's accident hit the papers as he knew it would be a big story in New York and the sports world.

Mr. Como immediately knew something was up. "Blake, what's the matter? You sound funny."

"It's..." Blake paused to catch his breath and wipe his eyes.

"It's what? Blake, what. Tell me!"

"It's Cooper. He's been hurt."

"Hurt? How? Where are you?

"I'm in Cooperstown."

"COOPERSTOWN! What the heck? How did he get hurt there? How did *you* get there? You were at the Yankees game!"

Blake filled Mr. Como in on the horrible accident and that Cooper was in a life-threatening coma. It was difficult for Blake because he had no one really to console him. His family was now gone, and like Amy, Cooper, himself, and his parents, they were all only children. Amy's mom was in Florida, and she had remarried after Amy's dad died—he and Amy hadn't seen too much of her after that. Mr. Como was the closest to family, so it felt natural to lean on his shoulder for consolation. Rudy, too, was like family, but Blake had no way of contacting him. He knew very little about Rudy's personal life, despite the fact they had become very close.

"Look, Blake, I'm going to close the shop and hightail it up there. I want to be with you and Cooper, no matter what."

"No, no, Mr. Como. You can't close up and lose all that business. Stay there, I'll keep you posted."

"Out of the question. I'm going to hang up this phone and figure out how to get there. You need me, and I need to see my boy, Cooper. End of discussion."

Mr. Como was frazzled. He needed to get to Cooperstown ASAP. He didn't drive anymore; in fact, he didn't even have a car, and besides, that kid from Brinks just told him his license was expired. So, he checked the train and bus schedules and found that the bus actually took less time because there were no direct trains.

It was the 2:35 bus that Mr. Como caught, which was a local; despite stopping in every Podunk upstate New York town, the trip was indeed shorter than the train. When Mr. Como arrived at the bus stop outside Sherry's restaurant, an empty taxi was parked next to the handicapped spot. Inside, the sole customer sat at the counter reading the paper and having a cup of coffee. It was George, the town's only full-time cab driver.

Como, in an almost panicky voice asked: "Are you the cabbie?"

"Yea, buddy, I am. Need a ride?"

"The hospital, please."

"Sure thing. It's only a couple of minutes from here. You from out of town, Mister?"

"Yeah, New York City. I'm here to see a friend who got injured. He's only nine years old."

"Oh, you must mean Cooper Anderson. God that was awful, he's still touch and go."

"You know Cooper? How?"

"Everybody in the world probably knows about that kid." George handed Mr. Como the *New York Post* he had been reading. "See!"

The *Post* blurted out in their typical reader-capturing headline: "Kid KOed at Yankee Stadium—Near Death!

Mr. Como read on: *The victim, identified as nine-year-old Cooper Anderson, from Brooklyn, New York, remains in critical condition after a line drive ball struck him in the head. The young Anderson and his father were medevacked to Cooperstown, NY, aboard the Yankee's official team's jet, to where Dr. Ivin Moskowitz, Columbia University's world-renown traumatic brain injury surgeon is currently doing a teaching sabbatical at Basset Hospital. Ironically, Cooperstown is home to Baseball's Hall of Fame.*

"Everyone knows everything here in Cooperstown. Well, I don't know Cooper personally, but I know Gladys and Gus. Mr. Anderson is staying at their B&B. They heard it from the horse's mouth, Mr. Anderson himself, and they told me all about it. A freak accident."

"You know, in all my years, I've never heard of an accident quite like this one."

The cab driver swerved to miss the flagpole in the center of Main Street. "Can you imagine? The kid and his father were sitting really close to the field and Bobby Evens hit a line drive that went into the stands and hit the kid right in the head. He was out for the count, and they had to medevac him here."

Mr. Como gasped as guilt filled him. Blake had told him Cooper was hit by a baseball, but hearing it from a stranger, his heart leapt into his throat as he thought, *It happened at the game, the game I gave them tickets to see. Oh my God, this is all my fault.*

The cab pulled up to the large marquee and dropped Mr. Como off. He had a small carry-on bag with him and the package that the Brink's courier left for Blake. He figured he deliver it to Blake as long as he was coming.

"Good afternoon; I'd like to see Cooper Anderson."

The friendly nurse looked up and smiled. "Cooper, you are here to see him? Well, he's in the ICU, and only family members are allowed. Are you a family member?"

Without hesitation, Mr. Como lied. "Oh yes, I'm his grandfather."

"Very well, sir, He's on the second floor, room 207. Here's a visitors pass, but you can only stay a few minutes, do you understand?"

"Of course, I do."

When Mr. Como reached the room, he peeked in. Blake was sitting by the bedside with his head leaning on the crisp clean sheets. He looked defeated and desperately lost. As not to startle him, Mr. Como softly knocked on the door. "May I come in, Blake?"

When Blake rose, Mr. Como got a better look at Cooper. His eyes were closed, and he was as pale as alabaster. Several machines were hooked up to his little arms, and he had an IV drip. Mr. Como covered his mouth in sheer dismay. "Oh my God, Blake."

*****

Gladys made room for Mr. Como at the B&B, welcoming him as they did Blake. After dinner, Blake and Mr. Como sat talking in the front room. That's when Mr. Como remembered the package that the courier had dropped off at Bea's and he went to his room and fetched it.

"Blake, this came for you while you were up here. I had to sign for it."

Blake took the package and looked it over. "It's from a law firm."

"Were you expecting something from them? You know legal stuff, maybe?"

"No, I wasn't." Blake held the box for a moment and abruptly put it down on the coffee table. A sour look appeared on his face.

"What is it? You look like it just bit you?"

"I don't know, but maybe it's something to do with Amy. Maybe these lawyers are handling her case and they found something." Blake was recalling that he had heard that a number of victims' families received personal effects found in the wreckage at the site. He read that they sorted through everything from wallets to cell phones to personal possessions. A cold chill raced up his spine. The last thing he needed was to deal with reliving that nightmare while dealing with Cooper.

"I'll open it later. But thanks for bringing it all this way."

Mr. Como visited Cooper the next morning. He spent an hour holding the little fellow's hand and telling him some great baseball stories. He didn't ask what the doctors said about Cooper's recovery. He couldn't bear to put Blake through that. But he did learn from the nurses that things were "stable," which he figured was an excellent way of saying nothing new.

Eventually, Mr. Como had to leave. He leaned close to Cooper's ear, sighed, and whispered. "You get better, little fellow. I expect you back at the shop to help me sort out all those new trading cards. Bea is making you ginger-snap baseball cookies. And don't worry about your daddy. I have his back."

Mr. Como pulled out a handful of the latest Topps baseball cards and placed them on the nightstand next to the picture of Cooper's mother. "I left you a load of cards, buddy, so hurry up and get better; you don't want the bubble gum to get stale!" As he left the hospital room, he kissed little Cooper's pale forehead. "I hope you can hear me, Coop. Now, get well; we're all counting on it. I have to go say goodbye to your dad."

He stepped into the hall where Blake was getting some coffee near the nurse's station. He had gotten to know the staff pretty well, and they were so supportive and accommodating, unlike some big city hospitals where the staff was too busy trying to keep up.

"Blake, I have to get back to the shop. But let me know if there is anything I can do to help. And, by the way, you're on the clock, so don't worry.'

"No way, Mr. Como. You're a small business and can't afford to pay people for not working. I won't hear of it."

"If you don't accept the wages, I'm going to tell everyone you know that you are a Red Sox fan! So, you better stop arguing with me."

As they walked to the hospital's lobby, he paused and welled up: "Blake, I'm so sorry. I'll be praying for my little buddy. Don't give up on him. He's a fighter."

"What can I say, Mr. Como? Thank you for coming, and thank you for loving Cooper as much as I do. I know your visit means so much to him." The two men hugged, each knowing that there was nothing more they could possibly say to each other.

The taxi pulled away leaving just enough time to meet the Greyhound 4:20 express to New York. Blake watched the car disappear down the block. He felt so alone and disheartened.

Of course, there were Gladys and Gus—his rocks. They supported him and gave him large doses of encouragement along with endless good meals and those famous cookies. He remembered his conversation that morning before he left to go to the hospital as he helped clean up breakfast:

"Gladys, I don't know how I can ever thank you and Gus. Without you both, I couldn't get through this. And don't worry, I'll pay you back every penny. I know you gave me a room that makes a lot of money for you, so don't worry, I'll pay you back somehow, I promise."

Gladys looked him in the eye, with the stubbornness of a mule:

"Blake, you will not. Gus and I are just doing the right thing, and you and Cooper are special. So don't even think about any paying back."

*****

Days passed, and it was late one afternoon when Blake was walking the halls of the hospital for just something to do. The staff at Bassett Medical had come to know and like him and allowed him some liberties. Blake headed towards the main lobby as a pair of elevator doors opened and two passengers walked out—one of them Lois Mason. She had just finished attending a hospital board meeting.

"Blake? Is that you? What are you doing here?"

Blake was caught off guard. The last time he saw Lois, it was less than amicable—his fault—but now that seemed unimportant and forgotten.

"Oh, Lois. Hello. I'm here with Cooper.... he...." Blake fought to hold back tears. Memories of how much fun Cooper and Lois had filled his mind and how Cooper often talked about going back to Cooperstown to see Lois.

Lois looked at Blake. "I've been out of the country, just got back. I had to bail my silly sister out of another one of her fiascos." Lois looked closer. "Is there something wrong? You don't look so hot."

"It's Cooper. There was an accident; he's here in the ICU. And not doing all that well. It's pretty serious."

Lois gasped. "Cooper, here?

"Yeah, he was medevacked from New York. It was an accident.

"Oh, my God," Lois recalled. "Yes, I heard someone was flown in for emergency surgery, but I had no idea it was Cooper. Like I said, I've been out of the country and out of touch." Lois looked at the pain in Blake's eyes. She, too, felt pain because Cooper had stolen her heart and was sad that, for unexplained reasons, Blake and Cooper and she became estranged. "I'm so sorry, Blake, really sorry." Despite how Blake had treated her, she reached out and squeezed his hand. "If you need anything—*anything*—please don't hesitate to reach out to me." Blake just nodded.

About an hour later, Blake returned to check on Cooper to find Lois sitting at his bedside, holding his hand. The color from Cooper's beautiful face remained drained. He looked so pale and helpless, almost lifeless. Shocks of thick blond hair peeked through the wide white bandages that wrapped his head. Blake looked away; he couldn't bear to see his once-energetic boy lying there.

His attention went to Lois, who was softly speaking to Cooper.

"And when you can, I'm going to get you into the Hall of Fame's vaults, where they keep all kinds of things that people never get to see..."

Still feeling awkward, Blake entered the room.

"Hello, Lois. I heard what you said to Cooper. That is really nice of you. I only wish he could hear you."

"Oh, I'll bet he does, and if he does, he'll hold me to it...you know Cooper."

"Yeah, I know, Cooper. I hope the Cooper I get back is the same one."

"What do you mean?"

"The doctors say there is a chance that Cooper's cognitive abilities may be damaged, perhaps diminished. They don't know either way. The brain scans are inconclusive. "

Lois looked down and fidgeted with her hands: "Oh, I see. Well, God willing, all will turn out well."

Blake scoffed and looked at Lois. "Lois, I try not to be cynical, but God gave up on me long ago. I guess it's because I gave up on him when I lost Amy. And now, with Cooper, I think God has it in for me, and I have no idea why. If you must know, I'm pretty mad at God, and I'm not expecting miracles from him for Cooper.

"Blake, let's take a walk."

The cool air felt good, and the couple walked several blocks. Lois decided to open up to Blake.

"Blake, you don't know me very well. I'm not the person you might think. I know all about lost love too. And deep pain." Lois took Blake's hand as they walked, not in a romantic way, but more for comforting.

"Yes, I knew love once, at least it seemed like love. A long time ago. And like you I was heartbroken. I met Devin quite by chance and at a time when I was most in need. My parents were killed in a boating accident, leaving me and my sister, Lenore, who is just fifteen months younger than I, orphans. After that, we were pretty much on our own. Well, not exactly on our own. My aunt and uncle were our guardians and technically responsible for our well-being."

"What do you mean technically?" Blake asked.

"I mean, the court assigned them as our conservators. But my aunt and uncle lived in the city and had consuming careers and a hectic social life that kept them pretty much occupied. They never had children, so parenting was foreign to them."

"Why would your parents ask them to be your guardians? They hardly seem qualified."

"Well, for one, they were close to my folks. And they were a lot of fun. My parents loved being with them, and we all traveled together and had holidays. In the end, I guess there wasn't anyone else, so they got the job. Besides, my parents were young and healthy, so they never expected to need guardians and the choice was just a pick. Not much thought was given to it. I don't want you to think my aunt and uncle weren't lovely. They were. They just weren't parents. They were pretty clueless. Let alone dealing with two girls who were grieving."

"Did they come to Cooperstown to raise you?"

"At first, they came, but later they moved us to New York. My sister, Lenore, loved being there, but it wasn't for me. So, there was a compromise. We would spend the summers here, in Cooperstown, and the rest of the year in New York or traveling around the world."

"Sounds like a pretty good deal to me," Blake commented.

"It wasn't bad, but, as I said, the worldly life wasn't my cup of tea. I turned eighteen, and then a year and a few months later, so did Lenore, the guardianship expired, and our parents' estate was distributed to both of us. That's when Lenore took off for Europe."

"So, she didn't feel the attachment for Cooperstown that you do?"

"No, not at all. She had tasted the high life in New York and was ready to do her own thing."

"And you?"

"I came back to Cooperstown and made it my home. A lovely woman, Mrs. Johnson, was a long-time family employee who moved in with me. She's still there after all these years. I love her."

"That must have been tough, being so young and on your own."

"It wasn't as difficult as you would think. Of course, I missed my folks and, like you, I know loss up close and personal. I grieved for years and felt cheated, bitter, and angry. But I learned to cope. I was always the serious one, sensible and mature beyond my years. I went away to boarding school and then college, and before I knew it, I was, well, 'all grown up.'"

"Wow, that's amazing. You were so strong."

"Strong? Maybe, or maybe just figuring out that life dishes stuff out and you learn to cope. I don't know if it was being strong or just surviving reality and doing the best I could."

Lois paused and decided to share an even more painful and private part of her history.

"You remember I told you that there was 'somebody' once?"

"Yes."

"Well, his name was Devin, Devin Daniels. We met in my senior year at college. He wasn't a student but a worker in the athletic facility. He was sort of a trainer but did odd jobs around the gym."

She sighed. "When I first saw him, I was mesmerized. He was the most handsome, strong, and take-charge man I ever saw. And, it's funny, I learned later that he thought so too. I couldn't help myself and took every opportunity to see him. At first, he didn't pay much attention to me, but later, he seemed to notice. When he asked me out, I couldn't believe it. It was like a dream come true."

Blake nodded.

"It sounds so silly when I say this today, but I became almost addicted to him. I couldn't wait to be with him. I felt loved and safe and desired. My life was wonderful. He taught me the physical part of love. I invited Devin to Cooperstown for the summer. He had no plans, and his family lived in Florida, so he readily accepted. That's when things started to change."

"Change?"

"Devin came from a low-income family and resented it. He realized that his incredible good looks and ability to please women, flatter them, make them feel loved were a tool he could use to his advantage. Devin knew I adored him, and he used my infatuation to blind me."

"Blind you?"

"Yes, in a way. Being young and in love, I let him, willingly. I came to realize that Devin was more interested in what I *had* than who I was."

Lois stopped to collect her thoughts. She wanted Blake to know this but worried that he might think unkindly of her or her foolish.

"I know this sounds ridiculous, but I was so smitten with Devin that I allowed the relationship to continue for a long time...way too long. You have to understand, he wasn't all bad, and when he chose, he was romantic and made me feel so special. Oh, sometimes I'd get upset and ready to give him up, but when he kissed me, I melted.

"He knew I was addicted to him, his charm. He took advantage of me. Eventually, I realized that Devin loved someone more than me, a lot more than me, and that someone was Devin. I eventually asked him to leave."

She sighed. "But I was truly devastated when he left. He took a piece of my heart with him, and to tell you the truth, sometimes I can still feel the void. After Devin, I vowed never to allow myself to be vulnerable, to be blinded by love, and never to put my heart on the line. No, I was done looking for love, it was too painful of a journey and the ticket for that trip was emotionally too expensive. Complicating matters was my inheritance, it was difficult to know if someone liked me for *me* or not."

Blake looked at Lois and understood. She in a totally different way than he, knew loss and suffered from it till this day.

"Lois, thank you for sharing this with me."

"I wanted to. You are probably the only one I ever admitted my foolishness to."

"Not foolishness at all. It was love, at least for you." Blake took Lois's hand into his. "You know, we're both a couple of broken hearts. Maybe if we were to put them together, there could be one."

"I've learned a lot of other lessons as I got older. I've come to see that money is not the ticket to happiness. Often it is the opposite. That's why I give so much of it away. It's why, honestly, I didn't tell you much about me when I met you. I just like being 'Lois,' not Lois, the philanthropist of Cooperstown."

Blake listened carefully as Lois continued.

"Blake, our bank accounts may be vastly different, but I feel far less fortunate than you because the one thing you had with Amy and still have with Cooper is unconditional love. And that alone makes you far richer than most people, including myself."

Blake was beginning to see who Lois Mason was. The couple walked down River Street pausing in front of Christ Church. Lois looked at the charming old building.

"I'm not a big-time holy-roller, Blake. But I do have faith. My life has been charmed but not without its burdens. The tragic loss of my parents left me feeling the same way you do. But in time, I came to get beyond the pain and loss and, yes, the resentment. That is when I realize that life is what you make of it and God's role is that he allows you to do so."

Blake listened.

"Until I forgave God for making me an orphan, I carried around bitterness, which is a barrier to happiness. When I finally was able to get beyond it, a tremendous burden was lifted. I became open to what life should be, what I wanted, and what I could make it be."

Blake contemplated what Lois was saying.

Lois pointed to the church. "I come here, not often, but sometimes. It's where my parents were married, and where they were laid to rest. Right over there. I don't come to pray but to remember. I believe everyone needs some form of spirituality, something bigger than themselves. Some call it God; others, well, it's just a feeling. But it works. It works because it gives you something or someone larger than life, to look up to and ask for advice or guidance. Praying is just that, asking a friend for help. I like to think of it as having a friend with powerful connections. When I feel lost or alone, I will ask for help. Sometimes I get it. Like when I met you and Cooper. It made me happy, and I smiled a smile that I had not for a long time."

"I get it. I had a great day with you when you showed us around. Cooper talked about that pink restaurant for a long time."

"Would you come with me inside? I'd like to ask for some help from a friend for you and Cooper, huh?"

CHAPTER TWENTY-TWO
HOLY SMOKES, ARE THESE FOR REAL?

THE WAITING WASN'T EASY. ONE DAY LED TO THE NEXT AND then the next, none with significant improvement. Bills arrived for Cooper's surgery and his stay in the hospital. Blake knew there was no insurance and that, eventually, he would have to pay the bills himself. Gladys and Gus tried to keep Blake's spirits up. Gladys would bake endless cookies and fix special meals just for Blake. Gus, whose day job was curator and chief appraiser for the Hall of Fame, would talk baseball with Blake.

It was a Tuesday night and Blake returned to the B&B from visiting Cooper. He was in his room and he decided to go for a run and was looking for his running shoes. Gladys picked up his room that morning and put his shoes in the closet on top of the package Mr. Como had brought from New York. Blake picked up the box and felt, despite his dread, it was time for him to open it.

The outer box was wrapped in brown paper, which easily peeled off revealing a heavy-duty shipping carton. Blake opened that and a pretty gift box carefully wrapped in bubble wrap lay within.

He thought to himself. *Well, this doesn't look like anything I expected. How odd.* A transmittal form from a lawyer was affixed to the box. He read:

To: Mr. Blake Anderson

From: Morris Underwood, Esq.

The enclosed package is being sent to you at the request of our client, Mr. Rudy Canter.

If you have any questions regarding this matter, feel free to contact me. My contact information is noted below.

The transmittal was initialed by Mr. Underwood.

"Rudy?" Blake thought. "I wonder what he is sending me. And why doesn't he just give it to me when I see him next?"

He opened the gift box and found another envelope. This one was pink. As he opened it Blake's curiosity was piqued because it wasn't like Rudy to use a pink envelope.

Dear Mr. Anderson,

My name is Marie Del Ponti, and I worked for Mr. Rudy Canter. It is with great sorrow that I report his passing. I was in his employ for more than twenty-nine years, and he was a really good man.

He died here in Palm Beach, Florida, just before Christmas, after a very short illness. Before his death, he gave me this package and asked me to make certain that his lawyer send it to you. He said it was very important that you and you alone get this, his gift to you and Cooper. I apologize for taking so long to send it, but after Mr. Canter passed away there was a lot to do. He had no family, and only the lawyers and I were left to attend to his affairs.

Mr. Canter spoke of you and your son often, and I know he thought greatly of you both.

Please accept my deepest condolences. May God bless his soul.

Sincerely,

Marie Del Ponti

Blake was taken aback by the news. More sad news, he thought, just what he needed! Although he only knew Rudy for a short time, he was a really wonderful friend. He was so kind and generous to both Cooper and him. It was really kind of Rudy to think of him in his last days. A bittersweet feeling flooded his emotions, and he worried how Cooper would take the news. He did know for sure that Rudy would be devastated to know that Cooper was so injured.

Blake carefully opened the gift box and slid out a lovely old navy-blue leather album.. On the bottom corner, the initials R.A.C. were embossed in gold leaf. As he held the album, another envelope fell out. Blake opened it and read.

Dear Blake,

You will get this after I am gone. It is a gift to you and Cooper, who share my love of baseball and all things related.

I want you and Cooper to know how much your friendship has meant to me. The times we spent together were among my most enjoyable. My only regret was that we met so late in my life.

This album is one that I have maintained for most of my adult life. Much of the content was given to me by baseball personalities I had come to know for decades while producing their uniforms. Other contents I acquired as a collector over the years.

So, my dear friends, please enjoy this gift. And remember, if you should ever have to monetize it to help Cooper or yourself, please do so without hesitation.

Thank you for your friendship,

Rudy

Blake looked over the album, which appeared to be old, maybe forty or fifty years old. He opened the cover and a yellowed tissue page folded back to reveal a plastic sleeve containing what had to be the most pristine page of baseball cards Blake had ever seen despite all his time at the shop and baseball card trading symposiums. The first three sleeves of the album contained, among other cards, a pair of 1968 Jerry Koosman/Nolan Ryan Topps, one card signed by both players. Blake knew that this was a really special set.

He turned to the second page, which had at the top, a pair of 1933 Lou Gehrig Goudey #160, one signed. By now he was in complete disbelief. On the very bottom of page three was a pair of PSA Mint 1953 Mickey Mantle Topps #82, again, one signed by the player. The majority of the rest of the cards were not among the rarest but seemed to be highly desirable and collectable. What made them especially interesting to a collector was that they were all triple mint, so fresh you could almost smell the bubble gum that initially surrounded them in their original package. And like the other special ones, they were in pairs, and each pair had one signed by the player!

Blake gasped. He couldn't believe his eyes. In baseball circles, finding this album was analogous to archeologists discovering King Tut's tomb. Blake also realized that this gift could solve their economic misery. The collection's value would be substantial and selling it could be the answer to their economic malaise. But it was a gift to Cooper and him, and it belonged to both, so the decision was not just his.

Blake quickly counted the pages, sixteen, seventeen, eighteen, nineteen, twenty! Twenty pages, each holding twelve cards per side. He did a quick mental calculation—480 cards....480 extremely collectible cards.... holy ravioli!

When the initial shock wore off, Blake thought about poor Cooper lying in the hospital unable to share in this really wonderful gift. He knew Cooper would be so excited to see the collection and even more excited to tell Mr. Como. All he could hope for was that Cooper would recover to enjoy Rudy's extraordinary legacy. Blake wondered if Mr. Como had any idea that Rudy was in the position to have this kind of collection. He also thought that it was really strange that he didn't even know Rudy's last name until now.

Blake decided to show Gus the collection. Getting an official appraisal would be mandatory, in the event the collection would be sold, and who better to trust for an honest one than Gus, a trained professional in the field. Blake brought the album down after he returned from the hospital one night.

"Gus, I was wondering if you would take a look at this collection. It was a gift to Cooper and me, and I was wondering how valuable it might be."

"Sure, I'll take a look." Gus opened the album and began to turn the plastic pages. "Holy smokes, are these for real?"

"As far as I know, they are. You're the expert; you tell me."

"Well, yes, I am an expert, and they sure look authentic to me. If you ever want to sell, you will need a professional appraisal, and I'm just the guy to do it. It's how I make my living."

"I was thinking, Gus, we are underwater with all the hospital bills and other debts, so maybe I could sell just some of the collection and let Cooper keep the rest, that is if he agrees."

"Sure, you can do that. But I'll tell you one thing, and take it from an expert, this collection will bring twice as much if kept intact, rather than sold off piecemeal. What makes it so desirable is that each of the cards has a duplicate and one is signed. I've never seen that before. Your friend, what was his name?"

"Rudy."

"Well, Rudy knew what he was doing. I'd say the collection is not the most valuable one I've ever seen, but it probably is among the most unique, and that, like I said, is what makes it so desirable."

"Oh, I see. You're probably right."

"No, Blake, not probably, I'm definitely right. Look Blake, do you trust me to take these into my office and do a rigorous authenticity review? It will officially authenticate the collection."

"Oh, Gus, of course, I trust you. I wouldn't hesitate for a second. And, of course, I would appreciate anything you can do."

*****

Blake's daily long walks down Main Street and back to the hospital were unbearable and filled with worries: Cooper's recovery, what to do about the collection, debts, and the future, all weighted heavily. Often, Blake would sit on the bench in front of the Hall of Fame's entrance and recall Cooper's gleeful face the first time he saw it. This was Cooperstown, and everyone knew everything about everybody. Townsfolk seeing Blake sitting alone would stop and chat, often giving words of encouragement.

"Mr. Anderson, dear. You look so desperate. May I sit with you for a moment?"

"Well, sure, but I don't feel like chatting."

"I'll bet you don't. You poor thing. We all know about your boy, Cooper, isn't it? Tragic, really tragic. My church group prays for him every day."

"Thank you, what did you say your name was?"

"I didn't, foolish me. Let me introduce myself. I'm Nancy Jane, and I'm the town librarian."

Pushing retirement age, Nancy Jane was a lifelong town resident. She had a sweet smile and meant well. She continued: "I hear that you are a friend of Lois Mason's; isn't that nice."

"Well, not a friend, more of an acquaintance. She has been very kind to Cooper and me."

Nancy Jane moved a bit closer to Blake. "I certainly would think so. She is kind to everyone, especially those who have hard times. Lois comes from a very wealthy family. Her family summered in Cooperstown for decades. Her grandfather and father, you know, were industrialists who made millions of dollars but never had a dime for the town. But when Lois inherited the family fortune, she decided to invest in Cooperstown."

"Invest?"

"Yes, young man, invest. You see, Cooperstown fell into hard times after the Depression. There was plenty of money in the town, but mostly confined to a few extremely wealthy families from New York, who came and went. Like them, the Masons lived on their big estate and, like the other millionaires, came and went on their private railroad cars, never bothering much with the locals. They brought in their own staff, so they didn't need local people, and they brought or grew their own food. Some summers, a bunch of them would even bring up an entire opera company from the Met to entertain their guests. They created a bubble that isolated them from everything. Sadly, they stayed apart and never spent much time or money in town."

"Sounds like a pretty tight class system to me."

"Oh indeed. They were part of the 400, the top socialites in New York, and we were from a different world. Until Lois."

"What do you mean?"

"Well, as I said, Mr. Anderson, Lois was Cooperstown's savior. When she took over the family money, she made it a point to elevate Cooperstown from a sleepy poor village to a tourist destination. She was so smart. She knew that creating a place for people to visit would bring money and prosperity into the town."

"Basic economics, I guess," Blake interrupted.

"The first thing she did was physically clean up the town. She bought up all the old and failing buildings along Main and Chestnut Streets and restored them to their original condition. Then she poured millions into the Hall of Fame Foundation, allowing it to build fetching buildings and museums. This created many new jobs and businesses supporting the growing stream of tourists."

"Wow. I didn't realize that."

"Oh, there's more, Mr. Anderson, lots more. Lois knew that the area had mediocre health care, so a state-of-the-art hospital was built with her investment. She used her influence and convinced the renowned Columbia University Medical School to partner in the project. Today, as you know, we have one of the best medical centers in the Northeast."

Blake sat silently, taking it all in.

"And then there was all of the artwork."

"What artwork?"

"The Mason mansion was filled with valuable artwork, many painted by New York artists, like those from the Hudson Valley School. Well, dear," Nancy, taking a breath, continued. "She built an entire building on her land just along the lake and gave it to the town. And then, bless her, she donated all of her art and funded a program to pursue additional pieces for the museum. And promoted some new struggling artists too. In just a few years, the building was filled with priceless pieces, many featuring the history of Upper New York State. She then got some of the most renowned museums in New York City to partner with her, swapping exhibitions back and forth."

"Oh, I saw that art. It is quite the collection. I had no idea she was responsible for it. There was no public notice as to any donors."

"Oh, that's Lois. She never takes public recognition. I believe she thinks it is gauche."

Nancy Jane opened a bag she had in her carry-all. "Want one, dear. They're delicious?

"No thanks, I'm not hungry." Blake really wasn't hungry, he was actually numb. Numb from the agony of the uncertainty, the worry, and the heartbreak, past and present. And a regret that he hadn't made the effort to learn who Lois Mason really was deep down.

"Oh, Mr. Anderson, you should at least try one. They are little tea cookies from Schneider's bakery, just over there. They call them 'thumbprints.'" Nancy Jane pointed. "You have to be quick about getting them, too, they sell out as fast as they are put in the case. Here, try one."

Before Blake could refuse, Nancy Jane was shoving one into his mouth. "Have a green frosted one, but I like the pink ones better, but both are yummy!"

Blake had to admit they were tasty. His immediate thought was that Cooper would love these. "They are good, uhm," Blake struggled to remember her name.

"It's Nancy Jane, and they are delicious, dear."

"Yeah, Nancy Jane, they are. A bit sweet, but very good."

"Oh, and speaking of sweets, are you sweet on Lois Mason, and is she sweet on you?"

"What? What makes you ask something like that?"

"Well, Nurse Regina, my friend, said that Lois visits Cooper almost every day. And that she arranged to have him moved to a private room in the VIP wing after the ICU. They say she's quite fond of the boy, so maybe she's fond of you too?"

Blake wondered how that room upgrade happened. He was worried about the additional cost, but the administrator told him there was no extra charge for this room.

"Well, that doesn't mean she's sweet on me or me on her."

"Of course not, dear. But you two would look good together."

*****

For more than a week and a half Cooper lay in a coma, his room filled with beeping equipment that monitored his every breath. Brain scans, one after another showed little more than the status quo. Blake took turns with Gladys and Gus sitting beside Cooper's bed. Lois would drop in several times a day just to see if there was anything new. Blake was happy to have her visits since she was always so optimistic and caring. It was like a little sunshine peeking through the dark clouds.

"Lois, you are so sweet to visit. I know Cooper would be so happy to know that you are here."

"Oh, Blake, he knows. I can tell."

"But .... he's unconscious, in a coma. That's not possible."

"Believe me Blake, he knows. I know he does. I feel it and so does he."

Blake was really beginning to understand something he failed to see before. But he couldn't quite articulate it, verbally or mentally. There was something....he felt it, just like Lois felt that Cooper knew she was there.

"I brought some flowers for Cooper. I don't know if he likes flowers or not, but I do, and flowers always brighten up a room."

"They are lovely Lois, thank you."

For a long time, the two sat silently, lost in their thoughts. Blake worried sick and Lois privately praying for that wonderful little boy lying so still.

*****

It was Monday night, just past nine when Blake called Gladys. He was beside himself and barely could speak the words into the phone.

"Gladys, this is Blake. It's Cooper...."

Gladys when she heard Blake's hushed voice, put her hand to her mouth to suppress a gasp. The worse passed through her mind. She couldn't bear to hear what Blake might say and called out for Gus. "Gus, please, come here, quick, it's Blake, and something has happened!" Gus, just as fearful as Gladys put his arm around her, bracing her for what could be tragic news.

"What's happened? Tell me, Blake."

"He's awake; he regained consciousness. The doctors are here, checking him out."

Gladys audibly sighed and repeated Blake's words to Gus. "He's awake!"

"Has he spoken?"

"No, but his eyes are sharp, and he moved his arms."

Now that Cooper was awake, Lois visited more often. At first, she would simply sit by his side and hold his hand. But as he became more and more aware, the two would sit sometimes for an hour or more and talk and even laugh. Blake would join in, and the threesome would have a great time. Lois often took turns with Blake reading *Leather Stockings*, a James Fenimore Cooper classic. The doctors were encouraged but reminded everyone that Cooper's recovery would take some time.

Now that Cooper was getting better, Blake told him about Rudy. He wanted to wait a bit longer, but he needed to get Cooper's input on what to do with the collection.

"Coop, I have something to tell you, some sad news, I'm afraid. It's about Rudy."

"Rudy? Did he die?"

Blake, taken by Cooper's directness had hoped to approach this with a little more subtlety. But he answered as directly as Cooper asked: "Yes, he did, Bud, he died just before Christmas, but we just found out a little while ago. He died in Florida—in a place called Palm Beach."

Cooper's eyes welled up, and he lay still for a moment. But the reality of the news soon passed.

"I've heard of Palm Beach. It's where all the rich people go in the winter. Half of St. Tim's grandparents live there, and lots of my friends go there for Christmas and Easter breaks. Do you think we could go there someday too?"

"Well, maybe." Not wanting to get off track Blake continued: "But I wanted to say that Rudy loved you and me very much."

"I know he did, he told me a million times. I'm sad that he died. I'm going to miss him a real lot."

"Me too, Coop, a real lot. I wanted to tell you that Rudy was very generous to us and after he died, he sent us a very, very special gift.... Some might call it an inheritance, or legacy."

"Really, like in the movies when the rich guy leaves all his stuff to his relatives?"

"Sort of."

Blake removed the album from his bag and put it on Cooper's bed. "Here it is, our gift from Rudy."

Cooper reached for it but was cautioned by Blake: "Be careful, Coop, it's old and valuable."

Although Cooper wasn't an authority, he still couldn't believe his eyes. "Geez dad, will you look at these? I've never seen anything like this, even at Mr. Como's."

"No, you're right. You wouldn't have. Mr. Como's store didn't have this type of collection. They're pretty special."

Cooper flicked a page, "It's awesome, really, really awesome. Rudy must have really loved us to give us this."

"I'm sure he did."

Blake was able to spend evenings with his son doing Cooper's new favorite thing: looking at and talking about the baseball collection from Rudy. Cooper was beginning to get up and walk around. His test results seem to indicate that there would be no measurable damage to his brain, which according to Lois and the doctors, was a godsend.

Blake knew he had to have a grown-up conversation with Cooper about Rudy's gift, and although he dreaded it he eventually brought the subject up.

"Cooper, we are so lucky that you are getting better, every day a bit more. You have the best care in the world."

"Yeah, Dad, everyone is great here."

"But this care didn't come inexpensively. The medical bills are mounting up, and all the other bills for stuff in New York too. The job offer I have doesn't start till fall, and to be honest, Cooper, we are in financial trouble. I hate to burden you with this stuff, but solving our problems requires your help."

"I'm sorry, Dad, and if I can help… well, I will. Do you want me to get a job?"

Blake couldn't help but to reach out and muss Cooper's now unbandaged dirty blond hair. "No, silly, not a job."

"Well, I will, Dad, if you want me to, I could work for Mr. Como, like you."

"I'm sure he'd loved that, but I don't think that's the answer. You see, the solution to our problem may be the gift from Rudy… the collection."

"The collection?"

"Yeah, Coop, the collection."

"I'm not sure what you mean."

"I had Gus take a look at it; he thinks it's worth a lot of money, enough money to get all our bills paid, and something set aside for the future. For if you want to go to college. Or if we want to move into a nicer place."

"And leave the neighborhood? Aunt Bea? Mr. Como? Mrs. Belinsky? No way!"

"I hear you, Buddy. But we still need a way to pay for the special surgeries you've needed. And selling the collection would be a way to do that."

"Sell MY collection?"

"Well, yes, Coop. But remember, Rudy left it to both of us, we're partners."

Cooper thought for a moment and another idea popped into his head: "Couldn't we ask Lois for the money? You said she has a ton of it."

"Of course not. That would be totally out of the question."

"Why? She likes me a lot, and I think she likes you too."

"Coop, just because people like you doesn't mean they will pay off your debts."

"Oh, I guess so. But Dad, Rudy gave us the collection as a gift; you can't sell a gift, right? Won't Rudy in heaven be mad?"

"Honestly, Coop, Rudy wouldn't be mad. Don't you remember, Rudy wisely said in his note that if we need to sell the collection for something important, it would be fine with him?"

"Yeah, sorta," Cooper lay in his hospital bed silently for several minutes as he pondered their conversation.

"You know, Dad, selling the collection would make me sad. It's something I love a lot, but I know about stuff like loss, like when Mommy died and then Rudy, which hurt and still does. But I'm getting over it, maybe better than you are. I knew I had to because you needed me as much as I needed you. You were, and maybe still are, so lonely and mad. Now, having to lose these cards is no big deal by comparison. I love the cards, but I love you more. And besides, I know this is just as hard for you as for me because Rudy's gift meant a lot to both of us. So, Dad, it's OK with me. Sell the cards. I don't mind; after all, what counts is that I have you. Who cares about holding on to this collection? You are more important."

Blake was humbled by the extraordinary reasoning of this little old soul.

CHAPTER TWENTY-THREE
EXTRAORDINARY REASONING

LOIS AND COOPER WERE BECOMING INSEPARABLE. HER GENUine concern and affection for the boy began to melt the foolish pride that kept Blake at a distance. He was lonely, and since Amy's death, no woman had caught his attention until Lois. He instinctively felt down deep that there could be a second chance for happiness, but it was so hard to let go of the past.

He knew he would have to make peace with the wealth discrepancy and face the naysayers who might accuse him of being "kept." Perhaps he could get beyond that since he didn't come to the table empty-handed; he was a Princeton grad who at one time was a big earner, and other than having to worry about taking care of Cooper, he could return to the big leagues. And then there was the collection, that could be a game-changer. He thought that the only thing that Lois's millions could not buy and the one thing she wanted most of all was a lasting and true love. Blake knew from personal experience that by any measure, this was precious. Maybe, just maybe....

Gus was invaluable. He produced the documents that authenticated Rudy's collection in time to be included in the Hall of Fame's annual memorabilia auction. Cooper was resigned to the sale, which made going forward easier for Blake.

The promotional material touted the collection as one of the finest in the auction's history and interest peaked worldwide. Collectors from all over filed into Cooperstown to attend the auction, and those who couldn't come signed up for phone bidding. Tensions rose as the auctioneer neared the time that Lot 234 would hit the block. Blake and Gus sat in the back of the auction room with their fingers crossed. There was no question the collection would go for a lot of money, but just how much remained to be seen.

"And now, ladies and gentlemen, I present Lot 234 …." announced the auctioneer.

Within minutes bidding reached a feverish pitch. Bidders would bid, and a split-second later, another bidder would increase the bid. A bank of phones on the dais manned by auction personnel would raise their paddle as phone-in bids were placed.

It was all over in less than nine minutes. "Do I hear any other bids?" called the auctioneer. "Going once, going twice, going three times, sold to telephone bidder 18."

Blake and Gus were astounded. The collection had exceeded the estimated selling price by more than 48 percent.

Cooper's eyes lit up to see his father walk into his hospital room, followed by Gladys and Gus.

Gladys packed a mobile feast to take to the hospital, where Cooper, Gus, and Blake waited. Cooper was doing much better and was hoping to be released by the weekend.

"Here we go, guys," Gladys announced. "Everyone's favorite. I got deviled eggs for Mr. Anderson, mac and cheese for Cooper, and Gus's favorite, smoked kippers."

"Ugh," Cooper sounded off. "Those look disgusting."

"Hey, Mr. Cooper, I got a bit of a surprise for you," Gus said as he approached Cooper's hospital bed.

"Oh, a surprise, I love surprises. What is it?"

"This is a secret surprise that not even your dad knows about."

Not having his dad know about it made it even more exciting. Cooper couldn't stand the suspense. "Come on, Gus what is it?"

Gus dug into his coat pocket and fished out a little black velvet pouch.

"It's in here." Gus waved the little pouch tormenting Cooper.

"Open it, please?"

Gus untied the string that kept the bag closed. He reached into the pouch and ever so carefully pulled out a small plastic rectangular object. "Here it is."

Blake and Gladys moved closer so they could see too.

Cooper strained to see and recognized it immediately. "It's a Joe DiMaggio rookie card, signed by him! Where did you get that?"

"You're not going to believe it, but when I was appraising the collection, I examined every page and card. I had to carefully remove them, one by one, and authenticate them. Many of the cards had duplicates, but this one and only this one was a triplicate."

Blake, Cooper, and Gladys, in unison, repeated Gus's word. "Triplicate!"

"Yes, triplicate. There was a third card hidden behind the pair. I realized that removing the third card from the collection would have no real material effect on the entire collection's value. So, old Gussie here removed the card and saved it just for my buddy Cooper. So now you will have something to remember Rudy by."

Cooper clapped in joy, and Blake slapped Gus on the back. "You old coot, you. Way to go."

While the new little family was celebrating their victory, Lois knocked on the door.

"Hi, everyone. May I come in?"

Cooper shifted his little body, sitting up a bit more, waving Lois in.

"Hi, Lois, you are just in time. Gladys has made a feast, and there's plenty," said Blake, smiling at her.

Gladys and Gus flushed for a moment. They had never met Lois and gave her almost celebrity status as they felt a little awkward.

"And you are Gladys and Gus, right?" asked Lois. "I know all about you. A little bird told me that you make the most delicious chocolate chip cookies in all of Cooperstown, including those at Schneider's bakery." Lois leaned over and winked at Cooper. "And Gus, I know of you. You're our best curator at the Hall. It's a pleasure to finally meet you personally."

Gladys glanced at Gus, and he glanced back. How could it be that the famous Lois Mason knew anything about them?

Lois shook Blake's hand and said: "Blake, I'm so happy for you. I understand that your collection did extremely well at the auction. This should be a tremendous relief for you."

"Thanks, Lois, But it's sort of bittersweet. The collection was a gift from a dear friend and having to sell it was a painful and difficult decision, but it had to be done."

"Of course, I completely understand. Some things in life are painful and must be endured."

Lots of laughter and joking emanated from the room, so much so that the duty nurse had to come in to see what was happening.

"My, my, aren't we having fun? But it's much too much noise and too much excitement for Cooper, so mush, mush, the party is over."

The nurse turned to leave and noticed Lois in the corner of the room. "Oh, Miss Mason, I didn't see you there. I'm so sorry. Please, all of you stay, enjoy, but keep it down a little bit."

Blake shook his head and thought that knowing Lois Mason in Cooperstown was like knowing one of the Rockefellers in New York. But then he thought again, she probably was related to them somewhere along the line. "Cooper, the nurse is right; it's time for us to go. Come on, everyone, say good night."

Cooper asked: "Dad, could you stay until I fall asleep, please."

Blake looked at the nurse, and she nodded her approval. "Sure, Champ."

CHAPTER TWENTY-FOUR
THE BEST GIFT EVER!

BLAKE WAS IN AND OUT OF THE HOSPITAL ROOM FOR SHORT visits two and three times a day. This evening Cooper was feeling really well and so happy to see his dad.

"Dad, Dad, I missed you. When can I leave?"

"Miss me, I spend more time here than most doctors. As far as leaving, the doctors want just one more day, and then they will release you."

"Great, great. Dad, I was thinking do we have to go back to Brooklyn? There's nothing there for us."

"Well, there's school and Mr. Como at the shop. Don't you miss them? Now that we sold the cards, we could get a better apartment, maybe a Mini Cooper too."

Cooper, beyond his years in maturity, shook his head in agreement. "Yeah, I liked it at St. Tim's, and Mr. Como is cool. But, Dad, you don't have a job. New York is so expensive, and the money from the cards can't last forever."

Blake shook his head, first in amazement that Cooper could be so astute, and second because he knew the kid was right. "No,

Cooper, I know all that. But I'm going to get another job. I have a prospect right now at another school, for the fall, not as a vice principal, but the hours will be the same as yours. You'll see; we'll figure it out."

"Dad, why can't we move to Cooperstown? I love it here, and I could be near all the baseball stuff and—"

"Cooperstown! I don't think so, buddy. Finding a job in a small place like this would be tough, and we don't know anybody."

"Sure, we do. We know Lois, Gladys, and Gus, and I know many nurses now. It would be great."

"I don't know," Blake said reluctantly. "It would be a big decision."

"And besides, Dad, Lois wants us to stay. She said so."

"Lois? She said what?"

"Well, I told her I wanted to live here, and she thought it was a cool idea. I really like her, and she likes you, and me too..."

"She said that?"

"Yeah, she told me that you are a really nice guy and the best dad, but I already knew that. She feels sorry for you, not because you don't have much money, but because you lost Mom and are so lonely. Maybe you and her can get together."

"Get together. Are you kidding? Look, champ, we are way out of her league."

"Her league? She doesn't play baseball!"

"Not that kind of league; I mean in her social circle. She comes from great wealth, and ... well, we aren't part of that."

"Oh, Dad, she isn't like that. She doesn't give a flip about any of that. I can tell. She is so nice, and I think she's kind of sweet on you."

"She said that?"

"Not exactly, but she said you must have been a wonderful husband because you are such a good father. Come on, Dad, give her a chance; all that stuff you worry about doesn't matter."

Blake changed the subject: "So what is the first thing you want to do when you get out of here?"

"I want to go to a baseball game."

"That figures."

"Dad, I'm a little tired. Do you mind if I close my eyes for a little while? But don't go away."

"Sure, Bud, take a snooze; your old man will sit right here next to you."

There was a lot to think about. Cooper was right. New York City didn't have much left for them. And Cooper's survival was a gift from God, so granting his wish to stay in Cooperstown for a new life should not be dismissed without serious consideration. God. He thought about Lois's words in front of that charming old church, the one her folks got married in... Christ Church, that was it. How did she put it? Life is what you make it, and God's role allows you to. Hmmm.

Lois said something else that hit home; he couldn't remember her exact words, but it was something about until she forgave God for taking her parents, she was bitter, and bitterness is a barrier to happiness. She said if you can get beyond that, a great burden would be lifted, and a whole new life can be lived. Maybe he was ready to allow himself a second chance; perhaps that chance was right in front of him.

But what about this Lois stuff? Was it Cooper pipe dreaming, or was there a spark? No question, he felt something, but did she? He remembered that almost-kiss by the fire. *What if,* he thought.

His conversation with Nancy Jane, the talkative librarian, was enlightening. Lois Mason was a local hero and was unlike the rich and famous friends and family she was raised with. She certainly wasn't like the rich grand dames of the women at St. Tim's. He thought, *you know, she's a beautiful woman.* A wholesome type, with kind eyes and an engaging smile. A smile much like Amy's. Amy, he thought, what would she have to say about all this? Blake knew that she would want the best for Cooper and having a woman in his life who cared for and loved Cooper would certainly please her. But what about him? Could he ever love anyone the way he loved Amy…? No, no, he couldn't. But, he thought, *maybe I could love Lois in a different way.* Indeed, he was attracted, no problem there, but …. But what? *What indeed,* he thought.

Was it time to bury the anger, to relieve himself from the burden of bitterness? Lois had told him straight: "Until you do, you will never find the happiness you deserve."

His thoughts were interrupted by a soft knock on the door. It was Lois.

"May I come in?"

"Sure, please do," Blake whispered. "Coop just wanted to catch a few winks. He still tires easily."

"Yes, I know. Sometimes he falls asleep while I'm reading to him. He's so adorable when he sleeps; well, to be honest, he's cute all of the time, even when he tries to convince you to do something you don't really want to do."

"I know what you mean. He can talk you into giving up one of your eyes and convince you that you look better without it."

"Ha-ha, you got that right. But I love him so much. He is sunshine on a cloudy day. If God had intended me to have a son, I'd want one just like Cooper."

Blake looked up. He didn't see an heiress or a socialite. No, he saw a beautiful woman with a beautiful heart. And this person, a good person, was someone that he could truly love, differently from Amy, but sincerely and fully.

Blake wanted to level with Lois; he felt the need to put his cards on the table.

"Lois, my life fell apart when I lost Amy, but slowly I've tried to put it back together again. I gave up my lucrative job to take care Cooper. I felt he lost his mother and needed a fulltime father, not an absentee Wall Streeter working eighty hours a week. So, my prospects for high earnings became and still are dim. The job at St. Tim's barely made ends meet, and even that is gone. Then the freak accident with Cooper happened, and I just about lost it. But then out of nowhere, things changed. Cooper survived, and by all accounts should be back to normal. That was a miracle. And another miracle was that my dear friend Rudy gifted us the collection. The sale gave us the security we so desperately needed. And, I know this sounds foolish, but being able to support my family is important to me."

Lois walked behind the chair where Blake sat. She put her hands on his shoulders and said: "These shoulders have carried a lot of weight for a long, long time: Losing your wife, nurturing and loving Cooper, providing a home for him, and the abuse of a jealous and vindictive principal."

Blake interrupted. "How do you know about the principal?"

"Cooper told me. He's like the town crier."

"What else did he tell you?"

"Lots of things."

"Like?"

"Well, like you hate housework, except on Saturdays, and that you are grumpy until you have your morning coffee."

"What else?"

"That you never want quarters and you wear briefs like him, not boxers, and oh yes, that you miss his mommy as much as he does. He knows because sometimes you cry, just like him, when he isn't looking."

"How embarrassing."

"Crying is not embarrassing!"

"I don't mean crying; I mean embarrassing that he told you I wear briefs.... God, can't a guy have any secrets?"

"Enough, now let me finish what I was saying. Those strong, handsome shoulders make you the man you are and the kind of man any woman would love to have in her life."

Blake looked back. "What are you saying? Are you saying what I think you are?"

"I'm saying that one must go with their heart and that nothing, not even pride, should stop them."

Blake stood up from the chair. "Lois, do we have a chance? We come from such different worlds."

"That is a notion only in your head; just open your eyes. I'm in the same world you are, and the world I will always want to be in. Maybe it could be with you... If you and Cooper will have me."

Blake was amazed that someone like Lois could be so humble. She was a person who could have anyone; famous, rich, influential, even a movie star, and yet she seemed to be choosing him.

Lois pulled Blake to his feet and looked into his eyes. She saw a man who she felt she could trust with her heart and a person she believed she could love forever. Blake put his arms around Lois and drew her close. For the first time since Amy, he felt something down deep. It was a wonderful blend of commitment and finding something dear. For the first time in a long, long time, he felt he had found a person who he could love. No, it could never replace the young, innocent love, which comes but once. But he felt down deep that this new love would be one that would last a lifetime. Blake embraced Lois and kissed her deeply, and he felt his broken heart piece itself together again.

CHAPTER TWENTY-FIVE
NOT SOCKS AND UNDERWEAR!

COOPERSTOWN WAS ABUZZ WHEN THE WORD GOT OUT. LOIS Mason was getting married after all these years! She had made her intentions clear; there would be no big fuss, no brass bands or jetsetters flying in for a gala. No, Lois was adamant; it would be a quiet and personal affair. The wedding would take place at Christmas.

Wedding Planner Cooper took charge. He wanted the wedding to take place in one of his favorite spots—the Pavilion, where the three cuddled in front of the fire and made s'mores. The three of them planned the entire thing. Four giant Christmas trees were harvested from Lois's property and erected on each side of the pavilion.

"Put one on each side." Cooper directed the workers. "Yeah, just like that."

Blake and Lois watched and decided to let Cooper call the shots.

"Now, Dad, where did you put all that green stuff? You know, what do you call it? Garlic?"

"No, Coop, not garlic, garland."

"Yeah, that's what I said, garlic."

Lois and Blake shook their heads and laughed, knowing there was no point correcting him again, so garlic it would be.

The "garlic" was strung from post to post, and tiny white lights were wrapped around the yards of the entwined juniper and blue spruce. Earlier, Cooper and Lois had picked massive bunches of holly from the bushes on the side of her house. A half-dozen bouquets were placed in large, galvanized milk cans at one end of the pavilion, forming a perfect backdrop where the couple would exchange vows.

One of the workers had made a huge boxwood kissing ball and decorated it with white satin bows. Carefully the men hung it in the center of the pavilion. At the base of the ball, two entwined branches of mistletoe hung down. When Cooper looked around the barn, he found a long red carpet used at horse shows. The judges walked down the carpet as they considered the entries.

When he saw it, he asked: "Hey Lois, would it be all right if we use this carpet? You can walk down it like it's an aisle. I've seen all the movie stars do that when they give out some kind of awards."

"So, where is that red carpet?" Cooper yelled to the worker.

"Over there," one of the men pointed.

"Cool, so let's roll it out so Lois can walk from the car to the pavilion."

Blake shook his head. "Where does this kid come from?"

Later, when all was done, the threesome returned to Lois's for a snack.

The next day, it was cold, but not frigid. It was Christmas Eve day—the day of the wedding. Father Wentworth, the local vicar at the Christ Episcopal Church, had agreed to officiate. He had known Lois and her family for years and was thrilled to be asked. The guest list was short. Cooper, as best man, Gladys and Gus serving as witnesses. That was it. Lois's high-society sister chose not to miss the season and ski in Zermatt rather than attend. A local harpist was hired to provide music.

The guests gathered in front of the roaring fire pit. Almost on cue, light snow fell, casting a fairytale atmosphere. Cooper was still in charge.

"Gladys and Gus, you stand next to Father Wentworth, and I'll stand on the other side."

Gladys asks: "How do you know how to do all this?"

"Oh, easy, I saw it on TV. *Father of the Bride.* Really funny too. But my dad isn't goofy like the guy in the movie."

Cooper had one more trick up his sleeve. Cooper had called Mr. Como in New York City without Blake knowing it and secretly invited him to attend. He had Mr. Como stashed away in the old barn just beyond the pavilion and beckoned him to come to join the guests. Blake was just arriving and spotted the surprise guest. They shook hands and hugged. Blake was so touched.

"I can't believe it. How…?"

"It was Cooper's idea. A surprise for you."

"It sure is. What am I going to do with that kid? He never fails to amaze me."

Cooper called out: "Now, Mr. Como, you stand next to me." Mr. Como moved over, but was cautioned, "Not there; that's where my dad will stand; go on the other side."

The Range Rover arrived, and Lois stepped out. She was dressed so simply and yet so elegantly. A long white dress with a lovely veil trailing from her pinned-up hair. It wasn't a designer dress from some high-priced bridal salon in the city, but one from the Smart Shop, a local dress store. She had discarded the bouquet that the florist had prepared in exchange for the single red rose that Blake had sent her that morning.

Blake was mesmerized as she walked the long red carpet toward the pavilion. The harpist played "You Raise Me Up," and all eyes watched as Blake's soon-to-be wife walked into his arms.

Blake's mind raced. After Amy, he couldn't believe that he could ever have another love in his life. But he was wrong. And he was grateful that foolish pride didn't steal this chance for happiness. He knew that in the end what mattered was not who Lois was, nor what she had. What mattered was that Lois judged him by his character, not by his bank account. With this new love, he felt freed and renewed.

It was a simple reception too. Gladys and Gus hosted the event at the B&B. The wedding cake picked by Cooper was his favorite, a fudgy chocolate Carvel cake. Gladys topped the cake with a plastic bride and groom she bought at Newberry's, the local department store, half price for $1.99.

After the reception, the threesome returned to Lois's house and spent the rest of Christmas Eve sitting in front of the fireplace, hoping that Saint Nick would soon be there. In the corner of the room was a twelve-foot blue spruce Christmas tree with gaily wrapped packages beneath.

"Dad, can I open a gift? You know, like we always get to open a gift on Christmas Eve."

"Ask Lois."

"Ok, I'll ask, but first, Lois." Cooper paused. " I have another question."

"What's that, Cooper?"

"Well, you know how I call Mr. Como 'Grandpa' now? Would it be all right if I call you Mom? You know I had one once, and I miss her, but now, maybe I can have a new one, just like dad got a new wife. I mean… if it's OK with you, and Dad too."

Lois's hand covered her mouth in sheer delight, reaching out for Blake. "Cooper, I would be honored and love it if you call me Mom. It is the best gift I could ever receive."

Cooper rushed over to Lois's open arms as tears of joy rolled down Blake's cheeks. He thought this little guy was a lot wiser than he.

"Cool. Now, can I open a gift or not?"

Lois looked at Blake, and he looked back at her. "Well…."

"Please, can I? Don't torture me? Please."

"Of course, you can," Lois answered.

"Great, how about two, you know, one from each of you? Please…"

They both know there was no use in prolonging the agony; Cooper wouldn't stop until they agreed.

"OK, Cooper, one each, but no more." Blake rolled his eyes at Lois.

Cooper circled the tree and spotted a box from Blake. And then he eyed another from Lois.

The tag read: *From Dad to Cooper.* He tore off the ribbon and then the paper, flung open the box, and jumped for joy. "It is the baseball glove I wanted, the signed one. Oh my God, I love it." He proceeded to run around the room punching the center of the glove like the pros did to establish a pocket.

He then turned to the other gift. He secretly prayed it wasn't socks and underwear, things that ladies love to give to kids. He recalled making it clear to everyone…no socks and no underwear.

"Open it, Cooper," Lois urged.

Cooper didn't need any encouragement. He ripped off the silver ribbon, carefully removed the paper, and opened the box. Neatly folded on top were three pairs of warm socks and three pairs of bright red briefs. Cooper fought back disappointment and faked a smile and held up one of the pairs of briefs.

"This pair is too big."

"Oh, I know, they're for your dad, so you can be twinsies."

Blake smiled broadly, enjoying the practical joke.

"Look, there's more, Cooper, under the socks," Lois said.

To his delight, he saw what it was. He couldn't believe his eyes. As he peeled back the tissue paper a beautiful old album was revealed, with three gold initials imprinted on the cover: R.S.C.

The end.

Made in the USA
Las Vegas, NV
14 December 2022

62528150R00134